REVENGE

CHRISTINE BESZE

Revenge

Revenge Series book #1

Written by Christine Besze

Copyright © 2019 Christine Besze

EDITING—Heather Ross, Heather's Red Pen Editing Services

PROOFREAD—Ellie McLove, My Brother's Editor

COVER DESIGN—T.E. Black Designs; www.teblackdesigns.com

INTERIOR FORMATTING & DESIGN—T.E. Black Designs; www.teblackdesigns.com

PLAYLIST

Zombie — Bad Wolves
God's Gonna Cut You Down — Johnny Cash
Close My Eyes Forever — Device feat. Lizzy Hale
Sail — DevilDriver
Breathe — Prodigy
Savages — Theory of a Deadman feat. Alice Cooper
The Sound of Silence — Disturbed
Closer — Nine Inch Nails
Scars — James Bay
Hymn for the Missing — Red
Sinematic — Motionless in White
I Am a Stone — Demon Hunter
Never Let You Down — Barnes Courtney
Cold Little Heart — Michael Kiwanuka
Rats — Motionless in White
Necessary Evil — Motionless in White

For Lisa and Christy! Thank you for listening to me whine and convincing me to keep going, even when I wanted to pull the plug on this. Love your faces.

PROLOGUE

Asher

I'M LIGHT ON THE BALLS of my feet as I bob and weave. My knuckles slam against the bag until they're sore. I feel every punch through my bones. Sweat drips out of every pore, but this is the best therapy after a long shift.

"Hook, uppercut, jab!" Eddie shouts from the side of the mat. "Focus, Detective Savage." His salt and pepper hair is slicked back. Everything about my partner is immaculate and in its place, from his perfectly ironed suit down to his pristine dress shoes. We couldn't be more opposite, but it works.

I ignore him and keep punching until the burning of my lungs becomes unbearable. Once I've exhausted myself, I rip off my gloves and grab some water. I swish it around inside my mouth a few times before swallowing.

"Here you go." Eddie hands me a towel.

"Thanks, man." I run it over my short, dark hair and the back of my neck.

"You need to bulk up. You're too lean." He slaps my arm and laughs. He's been telling me the same shit since we became partners a year ago.

"Wise ass." My mouth twitches as I unwrap my hands and shove the material in my bag.

Eddie leans back against the wall, crossing his feet at the ankles, and watches my every move. "You find out any more on that case you were looking into?"

"I found a few things. I'll do some more digging tomorrow and hack into their records. Benny is not smart enough to pull this off on his own and I doubt there's that much money in auto repairs. I know Diego's behind this. It has his stench written all over it." I toss back some more water before glancing up at the clock and jump to my feet. "Shit! Is that the time? I promised Lauren I'd be home early tonight."

"Take it from me, son. An 'I'm sorry' gift goes a long way with that." A corner of his mouth lifts.

"Thanks, but I'm not sure a gift will help put together the crib that I promised to build tonight." I'm scrambling to put my shit away and zip up the gym bag. If I don't get my ass in gear, I might be spending several nights on the couch.

"Enjoy your sleep while you can. Once that baby comes, neither of you will again." Eddie winks and tosses back his coffee. When I say nothing, he keeps going. "My youngest is twenty-three, away at college, and we still don't. She's gonna be the death of me, that one." He shakes his head and sighs.

"Thanks for the wisdom, old man." I slap him on the arm and head out with my gym bag over my shoulder.

"Funny fucker. Forty-four ain't old." He snickers behind me.

"Luckily, I've got twenty years before I find that out." Without looking back, I wave a hand at him and head to my car. "Later."

The drive is short and quiet. After I pull into our driveway, I grab my gym bag and the flowers I bought on the way home. Lilies are Lauren's favorites and always make her soften for me. Grinning like a fool, I head up our front walk.

The smile on my face dies when I find our front door busted off its hinges.

"Lauren?" Glass shatters. "Lauren!" I throw my bag and the flowers aside before rushing inside.

"Asher!" Her blood-curdling screams are like shards of glass against my heart. "Help!"

I race up the stairs two at a time and find a figure on top of my wife, punching her with gloved hands. A ski mask covers his face and he's dressed from head to toe in black.

"No!" Red consumes me. I don't think. I react. My body slams into him, tackling him to the ground. We roll around the floor and start throwing punches, but we manage to dodge each other. Whoever he is, he knows how to fight. During the struggle, I'm able to get one hand free and reach up to open a drawer from the night-stand next to the bed. I barely get my spare gun out before he nails me in the side. The gun falls to the floor and he uses this to his advantage. He's able to flip me onto my back, straddle my chest, and wrap his hands around my throat. All I can make out are his black eyes through the holes of his mask. My fingers are able to grip onto the cotton material and pull it off, but it's dark and I can't make out much of his face other than a jagged scar below his left eye.

The distraction is enough for me to loosen his hold, but before I can gain the upper hand, pain explodes at the back of my head. My vision swims as I fall to the side and struggle to focus. A pair of black military boots is the only thing I see before they kick me in the face, while the other person in the room takes my gun off the floor and tosses it to the man with the scar.

"Enough! Finish the bitch already so we can get out of here." The voice is low and muffled, but I know I've heard it somewhere before.

"What about him? He said no witnesses."

"Leave him. Boss has plans."

My hands shake as I struggle to pull myself up. I push with everything I have, but it's not enough. They buckle under the strain of my weight and I'm knocked back down. No matter how hard I try I can't reach her. The room swims in and out of focus behind a veil of blood, but her cries are all I can hear.

"No, please!" Lauren screams as a single gunshot rings out. Her shallow breaths fill the room like a knife in my heart, until everything goes silent and the darkness swallows me.

I'm not sure how long I'm out when I'm shaken awake and hear a familiar voice. "Asher? Can you hear me?"

My vision is still swimming in and out of focus, but I manage a slight nod. "Eddie? Where is she? Where's Lauren?" Each word comes out as a slow wheeze.

Eddie's blurry head shakes. "She didn't make it."

At his words, my world dies. Everything goes black. I'm numb and lifeless—a hollow shell that ceases to exist.

Nothing they say from that point on penetrates my hollow exterior. Not during my interrogation. Not during my trial. Not when they strip me of my badge. Not the pain on my brothers' faces. Not the words 'voluntary manslaughter'. Not even the word 'guilty' sinks in.

5 MONTHS LATER

PISS SEEPS OUT OF THE CONCRETE, BURNING MY NOSTRILS. THE clock on the far wall ticks by as it taunts me. Time is irrelevant here. Every second that passes is another that they own you—own every decision you ever make. You don't piss or shit without their permission.

No one has come to see me, but I prefer it that way. My brothers are waiting for me on the outside and that's all the assurance I need. Having them see me locked up in a cage would be an ugly reminder of everything I've lost, and I'm not ready to face that reality just yet. It will happen in time but on my terms. Everything will be on my terms.

The bars to my cell open and one by one we get in line, like ants marching off to the slaughter. We grab trays and take whatever slop they plop on our plates, eating it without complaint or we starve.

I take my share and sit at a nearby table without a word. In the months I've spent here, I've learned the hierarchy of things. Keep quiet and keep your head down, but take no shit either. The first day I proved I wasn't to be fucked with and I've been left alone ever since. I keep to myself and speak to no one except for my cellmate.

Carl has shared a cell with me for months and enjoys my silence, so we sit together as a united front. His dark skin is covered in tattoos that tell a story of the hard life he's lived. Out in the real world, we would never have been friends, but here we've forged a bond brought on by the need for survival. We have each other's backs and always will.

A loud noise interrupts my thoughts and my chin lifts to find Cyrus—the one pain in my ass—at our table. He flashes me a toothless grin but doesn't speak. His eyes never glance in Carl's direction nor does he acknowledge him. I'm not surprised. He's never cared for Carl because he's a racist piece of shit.

"You two fucking fags sit here thinking you're better than us, don't you?" He licks his top lip and laughs. "You want to suck cock, I'll pull out my dick right here."

My teeth grind together as my fists clench the sides of my tray. This bastard's been taunting me since day one and I've had just about enough of his shit. The whites of my knuckles should serve as a warning, but Cyrus has never been accused of being smart.

"Ignore him, man." Carl speaks for the first time since Cyrus sat down.

All eyes are on us and I know they're waiting, picking their moment to strike, like animals hunting for the weakest link and ready to pounce.

My attention focuses back on my tray and I shove a handful of what I think are mashed potatoes in my mouth. Ignoring him will piss him off more than me breaking his jaw. He's pushing to get a rise out of me, but I don't give him the satisfaction.

Cyrus grins like he's won. He knows he's getting to me and he thrives on it like the parasite he is. "You're a pussy. I bet your wife put up more of a fight than you."

"What the fuck did you just say?" My voice is low and hoarse from not speaking in so long, but the threat in my tone is clear.

He groans and the next words out of his mouth are my undoing. "I bet she had a hot, tight cunt, too. It's just a shame I can't fuck her myself."

I leap out of my seat and hit him in the face with my tray, knocking him on his back. Down it crashes, harder and harder. Blood coats my face as I hear his nose crunch underneath my weight. The rest of the prisoners take advantage of this distraction and attack each other. A riot breaks out, but amongst the chaos, I never lose sight of the fucker in front of me.

Months of anger and pent up rage are unleashed and there's no holding me back anymore. I keep slamming it down, over and over. Images of the bastard with the scar who shot Lauren replace Cyrus, and I bring it down even harder. The final crack of his skull snaps the last shred of humanity I was hanging onto. There's nothing left. I've succumbed, become the monster they've made me—one that's only satisfied by blood and pain. And make no mistake, I'm coming for every last one of them. Diego may have won this battle, but I'm winning the war. Vengeance will be mine, even if it takes my last breath.

CHAPTER ONE

6 YEARS LATER...

ASHER

EVERY MUSCLE IN MY BODY tenses the closer I get to the door. My fingers squeeze the strap of the bag that hangs by my thigh, reminding me that this is real. I'm not dreaming. I keep waiting for them to stop me and drag me back into Hell, but they don't.

The second I step through the metal gate, all tension leaves my body. Fresh air hits me in the face, washing away any lingering stench from inside. Sunlight beats down on my skin—a welcome invasion. I tilt my head back and squeeze my eyes shut, letting it etch its way inside me. Freedom has never felt so good.

Footsteps sound nearby, causing my eyes to snap open. Instinct has me reaching for my shank, but then I remember where I'm at and drop my hand back to my side.

"Savage." A pair of familiar hazel eyes meet mine, causing my upper lip to curl as bitterness settles in my stomach like dead weight.

"Rosenberg." His name sounds like sandpaper on my tongue.

His gaze holds mine, looking for any signs of weakness. I keep my expression blank, giving nothing away. If he thinks he can get anything out of me, he's dead wrong.

Deep lines crease the corners of his eyes. It's been six years since he had me locked up, and time hasn't been kind to him. "You may have gotten released early, but you'll be back."

"That right?" I plaster on a smile so tight that every muscle in my face aches. I'm not giving him a damn thing.

"Yeah, it is. I couldn't pin Cyrus' death on you, but you got lucky. It doesn't mean you won't fuck up again."

"Prison riots happen." My teeth grind together at the mention of that piece of shit's name. He got what was coming to him. I shrug to keep from saying anything that will incriminate me.

"I don't care what they say. I know you butchered her in cold blood." He keeps goading me, and this time it almost works.

At the mention of Lauren, my entire body goes stiff. My fingers grip the handle of my bag until the roughness of the material digs into my palm—pain the only thing keeping me grounded and stopping me from ripping out this fucker's throat. My nostrils flare as I focus on taking slow deep breaths. Going back to prison so soon isn't part of the plan. Finally, after a few beats of silence, I'm calm enough to speak.

He waits me out to see if I'll give him what he wants. When I step around him and continue on my way, he calls out, "I'll be watching you."

My steps never falter as I take a quick glance over my shoulder and smirk at him. "See ya around, Rosenberg." I hear him swearing behind me, but I don't give a shit. I'm a free man now, and there's not a damn thing he can do about it.

The sound of a lighter clicking open catches my attention. My brother's standing in front of his black pickup truck, a cigarette hanging out of the corner of his mouth. Neither of us speaks as he takes his time studying my appearance. I'm much different than the last time he saw me. I've packed on at least fifty pounds of muscle and have a shaved head. Tattoos cover both sides of my neck as well as full sleeves on both arms.

He exhales a puff of smoke and rubs his bottom lip with his thumb—a nervous habit he's had since we were kids. Nothing has changed about him, except he's a bit older and sporting a few more tattoos than I remember. Blue eyes that mirror my own stare back at me as he pinches the butt of the cigarette between his fingers and brings it away from his mouth. His dark hair is buzzed into the same military style cut he's had since basic training.

A few more beats of silence pass between us while we stare each other down, taking in every detail. He's looking for my scars, but he won't find them. They're hidden away where no one but me can see.

"You look like shit." He grins.

My chin jerks in response as a muscle jumps on my cheek. I want to say something, fill in the blanks for him, but I'm at a loss on what. The old me would have hugged him. This new version is broken and trusts no one. "Ax…" My voice sounds rough and dry. I wet my lips and clear my throat to try again. "Axel, I—"

He waves a hand out, stopping me. "I know, man. I know." He understands. There's nothing more to be said. His eyes flick down to my bag before his gaze comes back to me. "Let's get you home, big brother." His foot pushes off the truck as he makes his way around. I throw my bag in the bed of the truck and hop onto the bench seat.

My fingers rub against the black vinyl, taking in the newly done interior. Each stitch is done perfectly, sparking life into the old truck.

"What?" Axel glances at me from the driver's seat.

"I can't believe you still have this piece of shit."

"Don't knock ol' Willie Mae. She's been good to me." He rubs the dash like his truck has feelings and I just hurt them. "She ain't much to look at on the outside, but inside she's got everything I need." His lips curl into a sly grin. "You know how much pussy I got in high school 'cause of her?"

I shake my head and focus on the road ahead. I'm itching to put as many miles between us and this place as possible. Other than a few cars and the dead leaves littering the highway, there isn't much to distract me, but I do my best anyway.

Neither of us speaks again for the first hour of the drive and that's fine with me. It's a comfortable silence—familiar and safe. I remind myself that there's no more having to watch my back for what lurks in the shadows.

Out of the corner of my eye, I catch Axel staring. He grins and shakes his head. "You been taking steroids in there, man? You're fucking huge."

"Necessary." I shrug and steal a smoke from his pack laying on the seat in between us. The second I light it and inhale, peace washes through me.

Not much later, we pull up a dirt drive to a two-story cabin that's secluded and surrounded by nothing but Georgia pine trees. Windows align the front wall, separated by a stone fireplace and a wraparound front porch. Three wooden rocking chairs are lined along the front as well as a matching small table.

The tall figure on the porch walks out of the shadows and leans against the wooden pillar. Watching, waiting. His features are similar to those of Axel and myself, except that his dark hair hangs down past his chin, tattoos only cover one of his arms, and he's grown a beard since I saw him last.

I exit the truck, grab my bag, and walk toward the front door until I'm standing right in front of him. His eyes are similar to Axel's as they assess my overall appearance. I hope they're not looking for any semblance of the old me because they'll be disappointed.

"Zane." I greet him with a small head lift.

His stoic gaze meets mine. I stand there anticipating his reaction, and what I get shocks the hell out of me. A grin appears on his face right before he pulls me into a one-armed hug. My body goes rigid at the sudden contact before relaxing. Whether he notices it or not, he doesn't say. He releases me just as quick and leads me inside the cabin without another word.

"Welcome home, brother," Zane says over his shoulder.

My eyes dart around the room, taking it all in. It's a bit over-whelming to see it completed. Everything looks better than I imag-ined. They followed my blueprints down to the letter.

Axel and Zane keep walking up the stairs with me following on their heels. We enter the first open doorway into a decent-size room. I set my bag down on the bed and glance around. Other than the master suite, this is the only other bedroom on this floor and it's more than enough.

There's nothing inside but a small bed that's pressed up against the wall with a small blanket on top. My hand reaches out and shakes the bed, testing out the sturdiness of the iron frame. It doesn't move an inch off the floor. It's perfect.

I cross the room and stare out the large window. The view brings me a sense of calm. After years of staring at nothing but bars, this is a welcome change. "Looks good, real good." My knuckle taps against the thick glass. Nothing is getting through this. There's no balcony and it's sealed shut, but I don't need it to open. It's meant to keep things locked inside—keep them from escaping.

"Of course it does." Axel leans against the wall, wearing a smug grin. Good to see he's still as cocky as I remember. His thumbs are shoved in the pockets of his jeans as he leans against the wall.

"We built it exactly as you designed. Even bolted the bed frame to the floor." Zane never takes his eyes off of mine while he speaks. He's assessing my every movement once again, like he's lying in wait, ready for me to snap. Little does he know that I've become pretty good at hiding the monster inside until he's needed.

I nod and continue glancing around the room. The walls are as plain as the ones in my cell. Unlike those cement blocks, these ones are much thicker. "Soundproof?"

"The whole place is." Axel comes to stand next to me in front of the window.

"Good." I nod.

"Asher?" Zane eyes me from across the room. "You sure about this?"

"Yes." My gaze doesn't waver. I've never been more sure about anything in my life.

"But she's—" Axel's features harden as his body stiffens. He's growing a conscience and I need to shut that shit down before we go any further.

"A means to an end." My voice comes out low and lethal, brooking no further argument. Axel jerks his chin and walks out the door without another word, his loud steps echoing the entire way.

My eyes flick toward Zane, waiting for his response. Whether my brothers have my back or not, it won't stop me from doing what I need to.

"You've got something for me?"

Zane nods his head and tosses a folder onto the bed. "It looks like we have some hunting to do." His fist pounds against the jamb of the door a couple of times before he turns and walks away, leaving me to my thoughts.

I sit on the bed and pull out the contents of the folder. He gathered as much information as he could, but I'll obtain the rest myself. A photo slips out and my hand catches it before it can hit the floor. My thumb traces over the image.

It's all burned in my memory. Every freckle. Every scar. Her dark hair is longer in this photo, but her green eyes burn just as bright as I remember. It's almost a shame that I'm going to snuff out their light.

"Your time's almost up, little Charlee. I'll be coming for you, and soon."

CHAPTER TWO

CHARLEE

THE SECOND PROFESSOR MILLER DISMISSES us, I'm packed up and heading out the door. Two hours is more than long enough for me to listen to her drone on. I love art, but she's killing it for me.

"That was the longest class ever." Kelsey slips her book bag over her head and onto one shoulder. "If she didn't sound like a damn robot, I might actually stay awake more often." She shrugs, causing the mess of auburn curls on top of her head to bounce.

"You have a point."

"Besides, I joined this class for the nude models. When are we going to get to the good stuff? I'm dying for the chance to draw some real live peen."

"Can't argue with you there." I laugh and follow her out into the quad, her long legs making it almost impossible to catch up. Luckily for me, she stops to pull her phone out of her bag.

I take the time to enjoy the scenery while she does. Watching the leaves dance in the wind on the cracks in the sidewalk is something that has always given me peace—something I always used to do with my mom as a child. My head leans back, taking in the cool September air. Fall will always be my favorite time of year. The leaves are already changing color, making way for new beginnings and exciting possibilities. There's also something about the smells, late night fires, and wearing your favorite boots that make this girl smile.

"What has you smiling like a fool?" Kelsey hip-checks me out of my happy bubble and back to the quad where we're standing.

"Nothing." I shake my head and keep walking.

"Right. It has nothing to do with the fact that Colby Masterson couldn't take his eyes off of you the entire lecture." She tugs on my arm until we stop, and cocks her head to the side, staring me down and waiting for her words to hit me. Once they do, my world tilts on its axis.

"He was not." Butterflies somersault in my stomach as a blush creeps onto my cheeks. "Was he?"

"Believe it. The school's star quarterback was totally checking you out," she teases. "Professor Miller was droning on about line shading and his line was directed at you." She gestures between her legs and then to me.

I fidget with the strap of my bag and let out a nervous laugh. Attention from boys is a new thing for me. My father was over-bearing and had his men follow me all through high school, killing any chance I ever had at a normal social life. Doesn't mean Kelsey didn't help me sneak out a time or five.

"Hey, what are you doing tonight?" Her blue eyes cast me a side-ways glance. "That new club Orphic just opened up downtown and everyone's going to check it out." When I don't answer, she adds, "Colby might be there."

"Wish I could." I rub my forehead and sigh. "Not only would my dad kill me, but my English paper is due tomorrow and I still have a couple more pages to get done. It looks like another late night session in the library for me." My shoulder dips, adjusting the strap of my backpack.

"I don't know why you study so hard. You have one of the highest GPAs at UGA."

"And I'm trying to keep it that way." I want to tell her the truth, but I can't. She won't understand my need to get out from underneath my family name and the dark legacy that it carries. To her, it's something I should use to my advantage. To me, it's a curse that I want to run far away from.

"Have you even picked a major yet?" Her foot kicks at the grass that's growing through the cracks of the pavement as we make our way toward the parking lot.

"No. I'm going to focus on getting my Gen Eds out of the way first. Hopefully, I'll figure out what I want to do with my life before I finish."

"I still say you should go the starving artist route with me. Think about it. The governor's daughter and the criminal's daughter living it up on our own. It could be a real scandal." She wriggles her reddish-brown eyebrows at me.

"That's my back up idea," I tease.

"At least we have a plan." She shrugs but doesn't go into further detail about either one of our fathers. Not that I blame her. While she's carefree, it doesn't stop her dad from trying to run her life like mine does and since they pay for our tuition, we're stuck playing by their rules. Kelsey just pushes the boundaries more. "Rain check for Friday then?"

"It's a deal. We just have to keep my dad from finding out. He's still not happy about the last time we went out."

Her auburn eyebrows pinch together. "He does realize you're twenty-one, not two, right?"

"It's complicated." To say the least. Explaining my family to an outsider is never easy. Over the years, I've tried and failed to help Kelsey understand many times. She never will. Both our father's hold powerful positions in the state of Georgia. Mine just happens to be the one on the criminal side of things, which means I abide by a different set of rules than her. She's also too much of a free spirit for her parents to even attempt to contain. That's something I admire about her and strive to have for myself one day. I just have to play it smart until I'm far away from here—far away from the cloud that is Diego Vega.

"Well, we'll figure it out. Wear that green dress you just got. You look hot in it and it brings out the green in your eyes." She walks backward away from me and toward her car, flashing me a big smile the entire way.

"Only if you wear that slutty blue one," I shout back.

"You've got a deal, Vega." She winks and climbs into her car.

I watch her go before making the short trek to the library. Once I've made my way through the stacks and found my spot, I settle in. It's far enough away from other people that I won't be distracted, but also close enough that I don't feel isolated.

Flipping through the book, I'm on a mission to find random facts I can throw into my paper. Every English professor appreciates little details like that and I'm hopeful this will pay off in the long run. Well, if I don't lose my mind first.

Time flies, and before I know it, I've spent hours with my nose stuck between several books. I've been so absorbed in my studies that up until now I haven't even noticed that the tables are starting to thin out. Before long, I'm the only soul left. I'm coming to the last bit of information I need, but my vision is becoming blurry. I shut my eyes and rub away the migraine that's forming when a shelf creaks from the stacks behind me.

"Hello? Is someone there?" My eyes focus and take in the room. After several beats of silence, I shake my head at my own stupidity. "Nobody's here. You're just going crazy, Charlee."

My phone rings, causing me to jump and knock over a few books. The phone fumbles in my hand a few times before I'm able to answer it with a shaky, "Hello?"

"What's wrong, *Mija*?" My dad's gruff voice booms through the line. I should have known I couldn't fool him. Nothing gets past Diego Vega.

"Nothing's wrong. I'm fine, *Papá*."

He hesitates a second before letting it go and moving on. "Where are you?"

"At the library studying." I keep my tone neutral and glance around the room, making sure none of his men are watching me. He has eyes everywhere I go, so it's not out of the question.

"What the hell are you doing there this late?" A rapid fire of swearing in Spanish rolls out in one quick breath after that.

"I'm finishing up a paper for school." I sigh into the phone and fight an eye roll. He can't see me, but you never know.

"You still coming over for dinner tomorrow night?" He changes the subject to why he really called. "I miss you. Your mother does, too."

"Stepmother," I correct him. She doesn't deserve the title of mother. "And we'll see."

"Charlee." It's one word, but the warning is clear. Too bad I've never been good at listening.

"That woman may be your wife, but she will never be my mother." I've been saying the same thing for the past five years and it's been falling on deaf ears.

"Do it for me." My dad's voice softens, and he knows I can't deny him anything when he does that.

"Fine. I will see you tomorrow night." A deep sigh escapes me.

"*Gracias, Mija.* Dinner's at seven. Don't be late." There's no missing the smile in his voice before he hangs up.

I toss my phone on the table and hang my head in my hands. Dinner with my dad and his wife is the last thing I want to do. I'd rather shove razor blades under my fingernails than set foot in that house.

The sound of a book falling has my head shooting to the side. There's nothing there, but this time there's no mistaking what I heard. A sense of unease fills me and it's time to get the hell out of there. I pack up my things and do just that. From the time I leave the library until I reach my dorm, my pace never wavers. Quick glimpses over my shoulder are the only things that slow me down until I'm in my room and tucked safely in my bed. I plop back against the softness of the mattress. I'm so used to watching my back with my dad's line of work that I've become paranoid over every little thing. I roll my eyes at my stupidity. Old habits die hard, but I'm free from the watchful eyes of that house and I promise myself I will enjoy it. Consequences be damned.

CHAPTER THREE

ASHER

"I ALREADY TOLD YOU WHAT happened." I rub my temples as the bright lights beam down on me, causing my head to spin. He won't give me a damn thing for the pain. I know what he's doing. Making me sweat until I'm so tired I'll confess just to get the fuck out of here. But, he's wrong. Dead wrong. It will not make me say shit that didn't happen. I sink back against the cold metal chair and stare straight ahead. Being locked in this damn room has my teeth on edge. I'm used to sitting on the other side. Not the one being treated like an animal.

"Bullshit! You saw some other guy fucking her and couldn't handle the fact that she needed to get it better elsewhere." Detective Norris slams down the pictures of Lauren's lifeless body on top of the metal table. Ice pumps through my veins at the images before me, and I avert my eyes. "So you beat the shit out of her and when that wasn't enough to satisfy your ego, you shot her in cold blood."

I swallow down all my rage and anger, because it's exactly what this prick wants, and meet his gaze head-on. "You're wrong."

He leans down until I smell the coffee on his breath. "Am I?" His knuckle taps against the photographs but I don't take my eyes off of him. Those images will haunt me until the day I die, and I don't need to see them anymore.

Blood pounds in my ears and my vision narrows. I lose all sense of control. My fists clench and jerk forward, causing the metal of the cuffs to dig into my wrists. "I didn't kill my wife!"

"Ash? Wake up, man!" I jolt upright at the sound of my brother's voice, sending papers flying across my desk. My heart pounds against my chest as a sheen of sweat drips across my forehead. The nightmares have haunted me every night and haven't stopped. Being out seems to have made them worse.

I lean back against my chair and rub the sleep from my eyes. "Thanks."

Zane leans his hip against the side of my desk and crosses his arms over his chest, watching my every move. He's worse than the damn warden. Sometimes it's a pain in the ass how perceptive he can be. "You okay?"

"I'm fine." I shake my head and go back to glancing at the file open on my computer, feeling his eyes on me the whole time. Numbers and names blur together causing me to stare at the same line over and over again. My muscles tense under his scrutiny and I wait for him to call me out on my bullshit, but he never does.

He sighs and lets it go. Zane knows when to push me, and when to back off. His chin tilts toward the screen. "Find anything useful on there?"

I relax at his change in subject. He's letting me off the hook for now, but the look in his eyes promises we'll be hashing shit out soon. I ignore the tightness in my chest and answer him. "Not much. There's nothing directly tying Diego to Benny's Automotive."

"Maybe he used an alias?" His dark eyebrows narrow together.

"I thought about that, but Diego's one cocky son of a bitch. He thinks he's untouchable. There's no way he would hide. He'd flaunt it out in the open, seeing it as an opportunity to shove it all in APD's faces."

Zane scratches his beard and lets my words sink in. "Have you tried following the money? It might help to see where it goes." He leans in closer to the monitor and squints, attempting to make sense of it all. Judging by the look on his face, it might as well be in a foreign language. Give him a gun and he can have it disassembled and put back together in a matter of seconds, all while blindfolded. Numbers, however, are another matter entirely.

"There are a few minor discrepancies with certain accounts that run through there, but nothing major that stands out. Whoever Benny had doing the books was much smarter than him. Still, it doesn't explain the large amounts of cash he's been flaunting around. There's no way he can afford half the shit he has." I've been coming around to the same conclusion for hours and it's doing my head in.

"What about the drugs?"

"No damn clue. There's a connection between this case and what happened to…" It's been years and I still can't bring myself to say their names out loud. Not sure if I'll ever get to that point. "I feel it in my gut. There's more to this and I just need to keep digging."

"You'll figure it out. You always do." He pats me on the back and squeezes my shoulder. "How did it go last night?"

"I had Axel with me. How do you think it went?" I shake my head and light up a cigarette.

Zane gives an understanding grunt. Not sure how he's lasted this long without kicking Axel's ass a time or two.

As if he has supersonic hearing, Axel pokes his head in and takes in the two of us. "What are y'all doin' in here?"

"Talking," Zane says.

"Big brother telling you how awesome I was last night?" Axel leans against the doorjamb and crosses his arms over his chest.

"Hooking up with her friend wasn't part of the deal." I narrow my eyes, letting him see just how pissed I am that he went to Orphic without telling me. "Not to mention she's the governor's fucking daughter."

"Relax. You needed a way in. I'm happy to take one for the team and I didn't even give her my real name." His eyes light up like he did me a solid. He's such a cocky little shit.

"By getting your dick wet." I exhale a cloud of smoke in his face and stare him down with the same one I used to use on my cellmates to keep them out of my shit. Of course, he ignores it for the warning it is and keeps on talking.

"Have you seen her friend? Legs for days, face of an angel, and a sassy as fuck redhead to boot. She's the perfect package." He groans at the memory.

"Is that why you got jumpy and knocked over the library book last night?" I cock my head to the side, daring him to argue my point.

His face turns serious as he shrugs. "That was an accident. Things worked out fine. She didn't see me."

"You're lucky you move quick or else she would have." I shouldn't be so hard on him, but he needs to understand what's at stake here if he doesn't take more precautions. We're not untouchable like he wants to think. The thought of either of my brothers rotting in prison because of me is like a knife to my chest.

"Why are you on my ass anyway? You could have just taken her last night. She was alone and vulnerable. I don't understand what you're waiting for?" A muscle in his cheek jumps as he throws all this shit in my face.

"It wasn't the right time." My hand slams down against my desk, causing the computer to rattle. His words hit too close to home. I could have taken her last night, but a weird feeling—one I can't explain—stopped me. I'll be damned if I have to explain myself to him. I don't like being second-guessed by anyone. He keeps this shit up and I'm burning his ass with the cherry of my cigarette.

Zane senses the tension building and steps in before anything can escalate. "If you're thinking of changing the game, we have your back. We just need to know the new rules."

"I'm not. We're still doing it. Things just have to be in place is all. I've worked too hard to fuck this up by jumping the gun." I rub at the short hairs on the top of my head to soothe my rising temper.

"I don't know. Sometimes jumping the gun can be fun." The gleam in my brother's eyes gives away the direction of his thoughts.

"Ax…" He's being a serious pain in my ass.

"Whatever. I'm outta here. Got a hot date with a certain redhead." He flashes me a Cheshire Cat grin.

"You sure it's smart for him to get close to the friend?" Zane jerks his head in Axel's direction.

"No," I deadpan.

"You two worry too much." Axel shakes off my attitude like it's no big deal, but I can see in his eyes that it's beginning to wear on him.

"We have reason to." I pinch my cigarette between my fingers and stare him down.

"Name one." Axel keeps pushing the issue and I can't control how far I take this.

"Mary Stevens." That gets my point across but leaves a bad taste in my mouth.

All the color drains from Axel's face and his whole body hardens. "That's a low blow, even for you."

He's right. It was and I feel like shit for even saying it.

"Ax." I open my mouth to do something I haven't done in years, but it's my brother and he doesn't deserve my wrath. "I'm sor—"

"Don't wait up," he cuts me off. All I get is a hard stare as he walks out the door without another word, leaving me to feel like a complete fucking asshole.

"He'll be fine." Zane squeezes my shoulder, but it does nothing to ease the sinking feeling in my chest.

"I hope you're right." I run my hand over my face and let out a heavy sigh.

"Trust him. He's not the same little kid you remember. Believe it or not, we did grow up while you were away, big brother."

"How? He still thinks with his dick like a damn kid."

"Don't we all?" He shoots me a knowing look and walks off.

I try not to think about what he's implying and go back to my research. I've got enough on my plate right now. Shit will go as planned because I have nothing left to lose. And a man with nothing to lose is a dangerous thing.

CHAPTER FOUR

CHARLEE

I HIT ANOTHER RED LIGHT when my phone rings. My lips spread into a smile, as I see who it is. I hit the Bluetooth button on my steering wheel and answer it. "Hey, Kels. What's up?"

"I'm on my lunch break and thought we could hang out later." Horns honk as the light turns green, and I hit the gas.

"I wish. I'm on my way to dinner with my dad and stepmonster." It's a struggle to keep the animosity out of my voice, but I glance down at my right wrist and smile. I wore the emerald bracelet tonight, more as a way to still have my mother there for a family dinner than to piss her off, but it's a win for me either way.

"Ugh! He managed to sucker you into going after all?" She makes a gagging sound through the phone and I can't help the laugh that breaks free. I can always count on her to make me feel better.

"He did." I sigh, tamping down my irritation at how I can never say no to my dad.

"You're such a daddy's girl." Despite the issues she has with her own father, there's no animosity in her voice as she teases me. That's why I love her. Most of my friends in school couldn't handle who my family is. Not Kelsey. She welcomed me with open arms and never looked back.

"Sometimes that has its perks." I shrug, even though she can't see me.

"Fine, but whatever you do, don't tell him about Friday night. He'll never let me see you again if he finds out."

"My lips are sealed. I promise." I don't bother to correct her because she's not wrong.

"Speaking of Friday. Guess what?" Her excitement rings out loud and clear through the car speaker. I can't help but tease her.

"You finally pierced your clit?"

"No, not yet. This is just as awesome, though. I met a guy at Orphic the other night and he's meeting us there on Friday. His name's Shawn and he's got an edible ass."

"That's awesome, Kels." I keep my eyes on the road as I keep the hesitancy out of my voice.

"Why do I sense there's a 'but' coming?" She knows me so well.

"I just don't want to be a third wheel and kill your fun is all."

"Nonsense. You're my girl and any guy that I get with has to pass the BFF test of approval." When I don't say anything, she keeps at me. "Please. I need you there, Charlee."

"Okay."

"Yes! Thank you. You won't regret it. I promise." I can practically hear her jumping up and down through the phone.

"I better not." I turn off onto my dad's street as I tease her.

"Have I ever let you down, Vega?"

"No, never." I don't even have to think about my answer. She's one of the few people in my life that I count on.

"That's right." A mumbled noise echoes in the background and Kelsey grunts something back to them and then addresses me. "My break's over and I gotta go back to work but try to have fun with your dad tonight and we'll talk on Friday."

We say our goodbyes as I pull up to the driveway and wave to the guard at the gate. He nods and lets me through. The second I pull up the long drive, nausea churns in my stomach. I hate this house—

mansion is a more accurate word to describe it. It's oversized and looks like a small Spanish village, nothing like the average single-story from my childhood. This one is as cold and lifeless as most of the people in it.

I slam the car door and force myself to walk up the small walkway. Trepidation fills me with each step I take. The feeling only worsens when the front door opens and Marco fills the doorway, towering over me—all six feet of him.

"You're late." His tan skin contrasts with his white button-up shirt, while his black hair is slicked back with enough grease to start a fire. He's also doused in so much cologne it tickles the back of my throat and I fight the urge to cough. Some things never change.

"Traffic sucked." I shrug and do my best to ignore the way his black eyes do a head to toe inspection of my body. From the time puberty hit, I've gotten these looks from my father's men. None of them have ever made me feel as nauseated as he does, though. It's possessive and uncomfortable. When his gaze lingers on my breasts a little too long for my liking, my annoyance boils over. "You gonna let me in or what?"

A corner of his mouth lifts. "You always did have a smart mouth. I'd be careful. Daddy won't always be here to protect you, *Chiquita*."

"Is that a threat?" My green eyes narrow at him. He knows better. One word to my dad and he'll be swallowing his own nuts.

"Consider it a friendly warning for future reference." He does one last glance over my body, licking his lips as he does. A crease forms at the corners of his eyes, but he doesn't say anything else. We stand there holding each other's stares a beat longer before he opens the door a bit wider, allowing me just enough room to squeeze through.

I suck in a deep breath and slide past him as best I can without touching any part of him. One day I'll be free of this life, of men like Marco who think they're entitled to take whatever they want.

The second I step into the tiled foyer, I'm hit with a familiar smell. It's one embedded in my favorite childhood memories, a mixture of spices and warmth.

"*Hola, Mija.*" My dad wraps me in a hug and kisses my cheek before pulling back. His chocolate brown eyes light up against his tan skin when he sees my mom's bracelet on my wrist, but he doesn't say anything about it.

"*Hola, Papà.*" I return his affection as Marco watches on from his corner. I consider telling my father about the earlier incident with Marco, but he looks genuinely happy. These moments are few and far between and I'll be damned if I let a jackass like Marco ruin it.

"*Tienes hambre?* Maria made enchiladas. I know they're your favorite." He runs a hand through his wavy salt and pepper hair. At least my dad doesn't shellac his with grease.

My lips spread into a wide smile. Times like these I'm reminded of the dad I grew up with, not the dangerous man he's become. "Starving." I nod and follow him into the dining room with Marco trailing behind us like the dog he is.

We sit at the formal dining table that's big enough to seat twelve —my father at the head, me on his right, and directly across from me, the stepmonster herself. Her dyed blonde hair is pulled up into a tight bun and her makeup is pancaked onto every inch of her face, making her appear much older than she is. Marco walks past, taking his place in the corner and doing what he does best—watching.

"Nice to see you, Charlee." My stepmonster attempts to smile, but I have a feeling the latest Botox injection isn't allowing her to.

"Lola." I press my lips together in a tight line and nod my head in a stiff greeting.

The servers bring out the food, saving me from faking further conversation with her, and I couldn't be happier.

Dinner is silent and awkward. I hate it. It didn't used to be like this, but things have changed between us since he married his latest trophy wife. I pick at my plate and manage to eat a couple of bites before my dad breaks the silence.

"How's school?" he asks, in between bites of beans.

"It's good." Keeping my answers short and simple is for the best. School is *my* space, something that's not a part of all of this, and I want to keep it that way.

"Nonsense." He waves his fork at me. "You're passing all your classes with straight A's."

Dread fills me as I lean back in my chair and stare at him. "You've spoken to all of my instructors?" Damn him. This is something I wanted to do on my own without the cloud of my father's influence hovering over me.

"Sí." He nods, like it's the most normal thing in the world. "I had to make sure *mi niña* was in good hands."

I fight the urge to scream at him because it would do no good. He'll never understand. No one tells Diego Vega what to do, not even his own daughter.

"I remember the stress of exams. College was a tough time for me, too." Lola nods her head and attempts to narrow her drawn on eyebrows, but they don't move.

I snort. "College? Didn't you just graduate high school last week?" It's a bitchy remark, but I can't help myself. When my temper flares all bets are off and my mouth runs away from me.

"Charlee." My dad's stern voice should scare me, but it doesn't. I do have his temperament after all.

"What?" I toss my fork down onto my plate, lean back and cross my arms over my chest. "She's the same age as me."

"She's also my wife," he spits out with such venom I cradle my butter knife in my hand just in case I need it.

"Exactly. *Your* wife. Not *mi mamá*," I fire right back. *Why the hell did I agree to dinner again?*

He slams his fist down on the table so hard the dishes rattle, his chocolate eyes morphing into a sea of black. "Enough. *Tu madre*, God rest her soul, would be happy for me. Why can't you be?"

My eyes flick toward Lola to find a fleck of humor behind her eyes, and I realize I've just been played by Botox Barbie. This round goes to her. She has her hooks in him deep, like a venomous snake, and she won't be letting go anytime soon. This is something I will never get him to see, no matter how hard I try.

"Whatever." I roll my eyes and sigh. "This is bullshit."

"Careful, *Mija*. You're lucky I'm letting you go to school, but I can take it all away just as fast." There's no missing the threat behind his words or the reminder that he still holds all the control over my life.

All of the oxygen is sucked out of the room, making me gasp for air. The shroud of tension pushes down on me like a lead weight. I've had enough family time for one night. I toss my napkin onto my plate and fight back the tears that want to fall. "Speaking of, I have a paper to write. Excuse me." The screeching of my chair scraping across the marble floor is like fingernails raking down a chalkboard, but the faster I get out of here, the faster I can breathe again.

"Charlee." His gaze softens when he sees the hurt behind my eyes. "Don't go, *Mija*. Not like this."

"See you next week, *Papá*." Ignoring his pleas, I kiss his cheek and walk out with my head held high, but not before I see the cold smirk Marco gives me. It causes tingles of fear to ripple up my spine and I regret not telling my father about him.

Someday I'll be free of this life. Someday.

CHAPTER FIVE

ASHER

I T'S TAKEN ME A COUPLE of days to come up with a solid plan, but once Axel told me he made arrangements to meet the girls at Orphic, things all fell into place. I still needed more information to go on if I was going to get that slimy fucker Benny to talk, though. Hitting one dead end after another, I finally caved and called the one person I knew who could help me get exactly what I needed. Now, I'm parked at a curb in downtown Atlanta in the dark, waiting.

"I'm freezing my balls off, man. You could have at least stolen a van with a working heater," Zane complains from the seat next to me for what feels like the millionth time. He's dressed much like I am, all in black from head to toe. We're both wearing jackets, but I guess it's not enough for him. Even with a beanie on his head, he's still bitching. His complaint isn't without merit. It is unusually cold for Georgia this time of year, but my body must be too amped up on adrenaline to feel it.

"It's the best I could do on short notice." I shrug, never taking my eyes off the dark alley across the street. "Don't be such a little bitch.

You'll be fine." If he thinks this is roughing it, there's no chance in hell he'd ever survive being in the cage.

"So, who is this guy we're supposed to be meeting?" He cups his hands to his mouth and blows into them for warmth as he makes idle conversation to distract himself from the fact he may lose a nut or two in this cold.

"Carl." My fingers trace along the worn leather of the steering wheel as I fight the onslaught of flashbacks that are pushing forward. "He was my cellmate. He's the reason I survived inside. The shit they do to cops in there…" The words die on my tongue. I can't tell him the horrors I witnessed. It's unfair to burden him with my demons. The things I saw inside are worse than any imagination can conjure up and that's not something I ever want to saddle him with.

Zane goes quiet at my confession and I have to look to make sure he's still with me. What I see cuts me deep. He's staring out the cracked windshield, lost in his own head. "It should have been us who had your back out here and in there. We're family. We hunt together. We die together. Like a motherfucking pack."

"No. It was better this way. I didn't want either of you seeing me like that." It was hard enough having my brothers in blue looking at me like I was a piece of shit. Having to look at my own flesh and blood through the glass would have pushed me even farther into the bottomless pit of hell—one that I wouldn't have been able to come back from.

He gives me a disapproving grunt in response, and I let it roll off my back. He'll be pissed about it for a while no matter what I say, which is fine with me because I stand by my decision. It was the right one and if I had to do it all over again, I'd make the same choice every single time. Them over me.

Silence stifles us as my words linger in the stale air of the van. He won't ever understand my reasons no matter how much I tell him it was for the best. And that's something I can live with.

A figure moves out from the shadows of the alley and my hands itch with anticipation. I know who it is before he even makes it under the street light. I'd recognize that limp anywhere.

"I'll be right back." I climb out of the van and slam the door closed. I pull my jacket tighter against me as I look both ways and jog across the street toward Carl. The second I'm close enough he reaches his hand out and smacks me on the back in a one-armed hug. I fight the urge to tense up. We may have spent years in the same cell together, but touch is still an issue I'm working on.

"Hey, man." When he releases me, he takes a brief second to take in my appearance and I know what he's looking for, but I'm not a statistic. I will never be one again. Still, his dark eyes never miss a detail. "You look like shit."

"Long time no see." I ignore the dig at my appearance because he's not wrong. Between the late nights I've spent going over files, planning the shit with Charlee, and the fucking nightmares, sleep has eluded me.

"Fucker." He laughs and slaps me on the shoulder. "I've missed your ass. It's only been what, a couple of years?" He seems so different now, almost happy. It's a huge contrast to the guy I shared a cell with. Smiling is something he never did inside. Then again, there was never a reason to.

"Freedom looks good on you, too." I light a cigarette and let the nicotine distract me from the cold that's begun to settle into my bones.

Except for some new ink along the dark skin of his neck, he looks the same as when I saw him last. The only difference is that his hair is now down in shoulder-length dreads.

"It feels good, man. Wish I could say the same for you." He scratches the side of his face and watches me closer.

"Those are new." My hand motions toward his hair.

"Gotta give the bitches something to grab onto. Know what I'm sayin'?" He tugs on the end of one of his dreads with a laugh, and I shake my head. Typical Carl.

I let out an exhale of smoke and ask, "What do ya got for me?"

He hands me a small syringe and then pulls a manilla envelope out from the inside of his black sweatshirt. "This is all I could find without drawing too much attention."

I shove the syringe in my jacket pocket before clutching the envelope in my hand like it's a lifeline; in a way it is. "Thanks, man."

"Don't mention it." He jerks his chin in my direction.

"Right."

"No, seriously." All humor leaves his face. "Don't. I don't know how deep this shit goes and the last thing I need is for it to come back on me."

"That won't happen. I'll make sure of it." I give him my word on that. "We good?"

"We are. You have my number. Ring me if you need anythin' else." Just as quickly as he appeared, he fades back into the shadows under the cover of night.

I take one last hit of my cigarette and flick it to the ground before I cross the street back to the van.

"He come through for you?" Zane asks the second my ass hits the seat.

"He did." I rip into the envelope like a kid on Christmas. Inside are the clues I've been waiting forever for—the ones that will bring me a step closer to ending this. I pull out the photos and use the tip of my thumb to flip through each image until one catches my eye. Fire pumps through my veins the instant I zone in on the fucker's face. That scar is one I'd know anywhere. It's the one that haunts me every fucking time I close my eyes and hear Lauren's screams.

The shrill sound of my phone going off has me damn near dropping the photos. When I pick it up off the dash and read Axel's text, I almost do something I haven't done in years—smile.

"That Axel with some good news?" Zane narrows his eyes at me.

"He fixed the lock on the back door so we can sneak in undetected that way."

"Good." He nods, but I'm not convinced he's ready to go all in.

"You sure you're ready for this?" I'm giving him one last chance for an out before he crosses the line with me. Because once he does, there's no turning back, for any of us.

He holds my gaze as he answers. "Yup. I'm with you, big brother. No question."

"Good." I nod and put the van in gear. "Then let's go hunting and get us a doe."

CHAPTER SIX

CHARLEE

"You look hot!" Kelsey's jaw drops. "I knew it would match your bracelet perfectly."

"Thanks." I run my hands down the sides of my strapless emerald dress. It's tighter than I normally wear, but I love it and after the dinner fiasco with my dad earlier this week, I need a night of fun. "You look pretty damn good yourself."

"This ol' thing?" she teases and motions to her blue dress. The sweetheart-shaped bodice is barely enough to contain her ginormous boobs, and her red locks are down in soft waves, much like my own dark hair. My friend is a serious knockout. I just hope the spaghetti straps hold up better than the ones on her prom dress did. "I assume we're taking precautions to avoid the big bad daddio and his band of badasses?"

"Yes, and I'm leaving my phone at home. I can't be too careful." I wouldn't put it past him to have Marco or one of his other men use it to track me.

"Smart as well as beautiful. This is why we're friends." Kelsey grins as I lock up my apartment and follow her the back way toward our waiting cab.

"So, are you going to tell me more about this Shawn guy you've been seeing?" I ask as we climb inside, doing my best to ignore the stale scent of French fries that hits me in the face.

"I'm not giving you any preconceived ideas. You can judge for yourself." Her eyes light up as she glances at her phone. "They're meeting us there."

"They? What do you mean by they?" I'm going to strangle my friend.

"Don't be mad." The smile that flashes across her face is the one I'm all too familiar with. She's been giving it to me since the second grade and it usually means trouble.

"What did you do, Kels? Please tell me you're not setting me up on a blind date?"

"Not exactly." She winces at my sharp tone.

"What does that mean?" I toy with my bracelet to keep from wringing her neck.

"Well, I may have heard that Colby will be there tonight." Not buying that for a second.

"Oh, you heard, huh?" My eyes narrow. I wasn't born yesterday.

"Okay, fine. I may or may not have let him know you'd be there tonight."

I sag back against the sticky vinyl seat with a loud sigh. This night is not off to a good start.

"What's the big deal? I know you like him, and you'd never make the first move, so I did you a favor if you think about it." She shrugs as the cab pulls up to the curb.

"Yes, setting me up on a date without telling me is a huge favor. I should be thanking you."

My sarcasm isn't lost on her, but she just shakes her head and hops out of the cab. From the moment I follow her out into the long ass line, it's complete chaos. There are swarms of people everywhere.

"This is nuts. It goes all the way around the block. How are we getting in?"

"Leave that to me." She grabs my hand and struts toward the

bouncer at the door. Whatever she says has him grinning and glancing in my direction.

I tug on the side of her dress and ask against her ear, "What did you say to him?"

"Oh, nothing much. I just promised him that we'd flash him our tits later if he let us in."

My steps falter. "You what?" I cross my arms over my chest, as if covering them somehow helps. "No way. Not happening."

"Relax." She rolls her eyes. "I'm kidding. He's a friend from my Poli Sci class and I helped him study for a quiz. This is how he returned the favor."

All thoughts of our conversation leave me as we step inside. I'm transported into another world as the heavy bass of "Hysteria" by Muse vibrates through my chest. There's a purple haze of light that bounces off the black floors. Cages hang from the ceiling with a dancer inside each one. They move effortlessly with the music, drawing attention to their black bikini-clad bodies and matching thigh-high boots. The black and purple theme is continued throughout the place.

"Wow." My dad would kill me if he knew I was here, but this place is so worth it.

"Welcome to Orphic, babe." A smile lights up her face as she glances at her phone. "Come on." She leads me through a throng of sweaty bodies, up a set of stairs to a nearby table where a lone guy is waiting.

A cigarette dangles from his lips as he flashes Kelsey a wide grin. He's got a military essence about him. His dark hair is buzzed close to his head, bringing attention to his deep blue eyes. A couple of tattoos peek out from underneath his black fitted t-shirt, but it's the way everything else fades away to him except Kelsey that gains my approval. He's looking at her like she's his dessert, and my heart flutters. I'm envious, but happy for her all at the same time. Kelsey is an absolute sweetheart and deserves nothing less.

He kisses her on the cheek and then glances my way. "Who's your friend, Wildcat?" His southern accent has me going weak at the knees. He's the complete package.

"This is my best friend, Charlee. Charlee, this is Shawn." Kelsey doesn't take her hands off of him as she does the introductions.

"Pleased to meet you, *Charlee*." Something flickers behind his eyes when he says my name, causing my heart to stutter for an entirely different reason. I just can't put my finger on what it is.

"Same." I offer him a polite smile.

The music changes to "Poker Face" by Lady Gaga, and Kelsey about loses her mind. "Let's go dance." She grabs me by the hand and drags me onto the dance floor. Shawn stays behind in his seat, watching.

Kelsey and I get lost in the music. Song after song, we shake our asses. It's the most fun I've had in a while. All the stress of school and my dad fade away into the background.

I lose track of time, but soon the tempo changes to a slow sultry beat as "Closer" by Nine Inch Nails vibrates through the speakers. Kelsey and I share a look and go back to dancing with each other when I see Shawn come up behind her. He puts his hands around her waist, pulling her ass back against his groin, and dips his head down by her ear. "Dance with me, Wildcat?" he asks, just above the sound of the music.

Kelsey flashes me a look and I know she's worried about me feeling like a third wheel, so I let her off the hook.

"I'm going to the bathroom. I'll be right back." I'm a sweaty mess and need to clean up a bit.

Kelsey eases away from him and leans into me so that I can hear her above the music. "You want me to go with you?"

"I'm good. You enjoy." I gesture to her man who's currently eyeing her butt like it's candy.

"You know I will." She grins and turns back around.

I spin on my heels and stagger down the hall, toward the restroom. It ends up being all the way at the back of the club where it's dark and secluded. From the dance floor, it's pretty much invisible. This makes me nervous, so I pick up my feet and make it inside as quickly as possible. To my surprise, the stalls are empty. There was a line out the door earlier. I finish my business and do a makeup check in the mirror. There are only a few black smudges of mascara underneath my eyes, which is a miracle. I wet a paper towel and wipe any trace of my raccoon eyes away. Once I'm satisfied that I don't resemble a drunken train wreck, I toss it in the trashcan and head out the door.

Everything happens so fast that I don't have time to react. A hand is placed over my mouth and I'm tugged back against a hard body. I scream, but it's muffled by his hand and drowned out by the noise of the music.

In no time at all, I'm taken through the back door and into the parking lot. The cold air feels like needles against my skin. Dirt scrapes against my shoes as I stick my heels into the ground and fight against him. This does nothing to slow him down. I end up losing both of my shoes in the process.

My fingernails dig into his hand and claw at the skin, drawing blood. Knowing I made him bleed is only a momentary victory. He never even flinches, just keeps dragging me off to a dark empty corner of the parking lot.

"You'll pay for that." The palm of his hand digs into my cheek so hard that my teeth cut into the sides of the soft tissue. The metallic taste of blood fills my mouth, but I keep kicking my legs out as hard as I can.

We come to a stop in front of a dark cargo van where another man opens the side door. My heart pounds against my ribcage. I can't let them get me inside that van or else I'm screwed.

The one in front of me reaches for my legs, but I kick up and nail him in the nose. "Fuck! The bitch kicked me."

The guy holding me grunts and pushes my body forward against the side of the van, caging me in from behind. His lips move against the shell of my ear, causing shivers of fear to ricochet up my spine.

There's a slight prick in the back of my neck and the last thing I hear before everything goes black is him whispering, "Lights out, Princess."

CHAPTER
SEVEN

ASHER

M Y FINGER TAPS AGAINST THE wood of my desk as I sit in front of the many monitors Zane set up. Each one reveals a different view of the house's interior and exterior, but there's just one room that holds my interest at the moment. It's been several hours, and Charlee hasn't moved.

Dark hair fans out over the pillow as she sleeps. She looks like an angel, but I know better. Innocence is an illusion—one that's covered in the blood of the weak. The black lace of her bra clashes against her olive skin, only adding to her appeal.

Zane leans against the wall near the door. He doesn't say anything, but he doesn't have to. I can hear his thoughts from here.

"What?" I glance over my shoulder at him. I knew this was coming. Doesn't mean I'm at all happy about it.

"Nothing." His fingers play with the end of his beard and I know he has something to say.

"Bullshit," I grunt in response and continue poring over the new files I've managed to get my hands on.

"Sleeping better?" Zane flicks his cigarette against the ashtray and leans back, watching me closely.

"Yup."

"The dark circles under your eyes say differently." I guess he didn't get enough of a heart to heart in the van. He's pushing me for more, but I'm not in a good headspace to deal with any of this bullshit right now. Not when I finally have her in the next room and I'm so close to getting what I want.

The chair creaks from my weight when I shift back and meet my brother's gaze head-on. "What do you want to hear, Z? That I can't shut my eyes without hearing her screams? Seeing the blood seep out of her lifeless body as our unborn child inside her womb dies with her? Or how about the fact that I was locked up like a fucking animal with the very same bastards I put there, and they left me to rot like I was one of them? I had to fight every day—every fucking day—to prove that I was no one's bitch, or I'd wind up with a few dicks shoved up my ass. Because I sure as shit don't want to remember any of that." Blood pounds in my ears as I struggle to keep my breath steady. The demons are fighting their way to the forefront of my mind and it's taking everything I have to keep them at bay. I toss back some whiskey, relishing in the afterburn. Pain is my new friend. I've learned to live there, to thrive in the darkness and never look back.

Zane's quiet a minute; no doubt digesting every pile of shit I just dumped on him. "Not saying that what you went through was a cake walk. Hell, I can't imagine half the shit you went through in there. What happened to you and Lauren wasn't easy. For any of us. I'm just worried about you, brother. You're so set on revenge and making sure they pay for it, as they should, that I'm worried you're not seeing the consequences. Next to Axel, you're all I've got, and I'll be damned if you're taken away again."

"Not gonna happen. The only way I'm going back is in a body bag. There's no fucking way I'm going to spend the rest of my life behind bars." Just the thought of being locked back up has me ready to crawl out of my skin. No, this time I'm going down on my terms, not theirs.

"Fair enough." Zane straightens the mess of hair on the top of his head.

"Right." I shake my head and glance back at Charlee's sleeping form.

Zane does the same but frowns. "You sure that shit Carl gave you is any good?"

"I'm sure." At least I hope I am. She hasn't moved from her spot since I last checked on her. *What if I gave her too much?* She's smaller in person than I originally thought and I need her alive, for now anyway. My plan won't work if she's dead.

"Pictures don't do her justice." Zane whistles as he leans in a bit closer for a better view. I ignore him and focus on the files in front of me. Now that I have pictures, I have a better idea of how to handle Benny.

"She's not your concern." My temper flares back up. The thought of either of my brothers near her is enough to set my teeth on edge.

He holds his hands up in mock surrender. "Easy, big brother. I'm just looking."

A muscle ticks in my cheek. "Make sure that's all you do." I don't even like him doing that much.

"Something I should know?" Zane cocks an eyebrow at me, and it takes everything I have to not punch that smug look off his face.

"Nope. Stay away from her. That's all." I ignore him and go back to thumbing through the files, planning my next move. Diego will know that she's missing soon enough and things will be set in motion. Everything is coming together perfectly.

"Tell that to Axel." He slaps me on the back and blows out a cloud of smoke.

"When's he getting back anyhow?" I change the subject once again, before I lose my shit and do something stupid like putting my fist through my brother's face.

"Don't know. He didn't say. My guess is he'll probably be a while." Zane takes another hit of his cigarette and shrugs.

"Let me know when he gets back. I want to pay Benny a visit and show him these photos soon." I wipe my hand down my face and do my best to shake off the stupidity that is my youngest brother. It doesn't matter to me where he sticks his dick as long as none of it comes back on me.

"Axel knows how important this is to you, Ash. He won't do anything to jeopardize it. He's just reaping the rewards of being the helpful brother." He pats me on the back and walks out, leaving me to my thoughts.

I attempt to glance over the files once more, but I can't get Zane's earlier words out of my head. He's right; this isn't just about what happened to me. It's about all of us. I wasn't the only one to be affected. Losing our parents while I was locked up only added to the shit storm. Movement catches my eye, dragging my attention back to the monitor.

Charlee's finally starting to stir and anticipation churns in my gut. Someone's going to pay, but it won't be me. Not this time. I have the devil's daughter at my door and it's time to play.

CHAPTER
EIGHT

CHARLEE

S UNLIGHT BEATS DOWN ON MY face. My head pounds as I struggle
to sit up. The inside of my mouth feels like sandpaper. I attempt
to swallow, but it does little to help this feeling go away. I'm tucked in
on my side, taking in the room. There's a wooden door to my left
that has no knob, and I'm surrounded by bare white walls. Across
from the bed, there's a doorway that leads to what looks like a small
bathroom.

At the foot of the bed, there's a floor to ceiling window. I push
off my elbows to a sitting position and swing my legs down until the
tips of my toes almost touch the floor. I hop down and do my best to
walk, but the room spins. My hands reach out and brace against the
mattress until my vision comes back into focus. It takes me a couple
of tries to gain a sense of balance before I can stand all the way
upright and not fall over.

Air hits my skin and my blood runs cold. I glance down to find
that my dress is gone. I'm in nothing but my black lace bra and
matching thong panties. My eyes squeeze shut as tears pool in my

eyes. My mom's bracelet is gone. The bastards took everything from me and left me almost completely naked. It kills me, but the need to escape takes over and all else is forgotten. I focus back on the window and getting the hell out of here.

The cold wooden floor is like thousands of tiny needles stabbing the bottoms of my bare feet as I stumble toward it. Each step is harder than the last. Every muscle in my body feels sore and exhausted. It takes everything I have to keep going, but just a little further and I'm there.

My hands press up against the glass, letting the coolness wash over me, and I take a minute to gain my balance. There's nothing but trees as far as I can see. An anxious feeling settles in the bottom of my stomach like a lead weight. Being so far away from civilization can mean only one thing. This was planned. Even if I somehow managed to escape, I could get lost and die from the elements. Images of my rotting corpse being feasted on by flies floods my mind, causing a shiver to wrack through me. It's not a pleasant thought, but it's still a chance I'm willing to take. I slam my hands against the window with everything I have trying to break through.

"That glass is over an inch thick." I jump and spin around at the sound of a deep voice vibrating through the room behind me.

Leaning against the open door is my captor. He's tall, well over six feet, and towers over my five-foot-two frame, with the looks of a damn model. His prominent nose is slightly crooked, like it's been broken more than a few times. He has a head of dark hair that's shaved close to his head. Tattoos cover him from the neck down and there's a light dusting of dark stubble along his perfectly chiseled jaw. His arms are crossed over his chest, drawing my eyes to the huge bulge of muscle on his biceps. He could snap me in half with one finger and not even break a sweat. His eyes travel down my body, assessing me without an ounce of emotion. Inside I'm trembling, but on the outside, I am my father's daughter. To show weakness is a loss of power and I won't give him the satisfaction of having that type of control over me.

His attention drifts elsewhere and I take full advantage of the distraction. I run past him toward the open doorway—toward freedom, but he's much faster. His hand strikes out and grabs me by the throat. Before I can blink, he has me shoved up against the wall, so high that my feet dangle above the floor. My head jerks back with a loud thump from the brute force and his fingers squeeze down, biting into the flesh along the sides of my neck. A wince escapes me at the sudden burst of pain, but I breathe through it. Both of my hands are trapped between our bodies, rendering me helpless. I can't move an inch. He has me completely caged in.

My chest heaves as we stare each other down. Up close, he's even more frightening. There's a hard, rough edge to his features—one that's etched into every line of his skin. He's so close that I can see every scar on his face, every indent that gives away part of his story. The warmth of his breath—a mixture of whiskey and tobacco—brushes against my cheek. Our gazes lock, and all of the air is sucked out of the room. The blue pools of fire reflect back at me with a void, a darkness I've only seen on one other man—my father.

The roughness of his jeans digs into my legs, reminding me that I'm in nothing but my underwear. "Where are my clothes? And where the fuck is my bracelet?"

A corner of his mouth lifts into a sneer. He looks down on me as if I'm nothing more than an annoyance—a nuisance to be toyed with at his leisure. Anger flares up inside of me. I swing my leg forward and attempt to kick him in his balls, but he blocks it with his free hand.

His fingers squeeze around my throat a fraction tighter, cutting off my air supply; a reminder that he's in charge. "Time for the rules, Princess." He spits out that nickname like it's poison on his tongue. "Anything you want, you have to earn. Misbehave and you will be punished. And make no mistake, I can take anything I want from you. You don't eat, sleep, or even breathe without my say so."

I lose all sanity. It's the only explanation as to why I spit in his face. His jaw clenches, but that's the only sign I'm given that he's affected by this. He drags his hand across his cheek to wipe it away. Never breaking eye contact, he sucks my saliva from his tattooed fingers. My eyes linger on the ink that disappears inside his mouth as his cheeks hollow out from the suction.

"That was your one and only free pass. I own you now." His thumb traces along the side of my neck, over my racing pulse, as his hand clamps down even harder. The pressure increases until my vision starts to fade into a cloud of black.

Panic takes over and I fight back with everything I have. My nails dig into the exposed skin of his chest, but my efforts are in vain. He's too strong.

His face leans in until I can feel the tiny hairs on his cheek scraping against mine. "Remember that." He loosens his grip but doesn't release me. His body stays snugly pressed up against mine.

I suck in a gust of air so deep my lungs burn, but I never break eye contact. "My father will come for me."

He flinches at the mention of my father. It's a slight one, but it's there nonetheless. He releases me from his grasp and my feet slam down against the floor so hard that I have to brace my hands against the wall to keep from falling over. He steps away, putting some much needed distance between us.

"I'm counting on it." His eyes do one last assessing glance over me before he turns and walks away.

I'm braced against the wall, rubbing at my aching throat and fighting the panic that wants to overtake me. I've woken up in a living nightmare.

The slamming of the door knocks me out of my shock. I run toward it, but I'm too late. The deadbolt clicks from the outside, locking me back in my cage.

I pound against the door until my knuckles crack and bleed. Splinters cover my skin, but I keep at it until I lose my voice. The need to escape is greater than the pain ricocheting up my arm. It's just too bad that my efforts are in vain. He never comes back. No one does. I'm forgotten, left here all alone to suffer an unknown fate.

My legs buckle from the exertion. I slide down the door onto the floor and hug my knees tightly to my chest. Tears spill down my dirty cheeks, over my knees. It's finally happened. The sins of my father have fallen on to me.

CHAPTER NINE

ASHER

BLOOD POUNDS IN MY EARS as my pulse races. I lean my head back against the door and exhale. She has more fight in her than I was expecting.

My body vibrates with every pound of her fists against the door. It's solid wood and there's no way she'll be able to break through it. Still doesn't stop her from beating the shit out of it, though. She continues to scream obscenities at me in both English and Spanish.

The longer I listen, the more my mind fucks with me. Soon, her voice morphs into a different one—one that's painfully familiar.

"Asher!"

My eyes squeeze shut as the sounds take me back to that night. An ache cracks in my chest and spreads all the way down to my gut.

"Help me, please!"

I grind my teeth until they crack under the pressure. "No!" She's not Lauren. She will never be her. I push off the door and head down to the basement. If I don't blow off some steam, I'm going to lose my shit.

The gym isn't much. It's equipped with the basics, but that's all I need. Spending time in a six-by-eight cell has made such amenities unnecessary. I whip off my shirt and toss it to the floor before I wrap up my hands and forgo the gloves. I want to feel the very moment my knuckles crack and bleed.

The moment I step up to the bag, I can feel the tension that's coiled inside of me snap. I hold my hands up and assume the boxing stance with my left foot forward and my knees slightly bent. The first time my fist connects with the bag a fire from deep inside of me is ignited. It's been too long since I've punched out my frustration and I didn't realize until now how much I need this release.

With each punch, I let it all go. All of the pent up aggression from seeing the photos fades into a distant memory the more into it I get. Punch after punch, it all falls away. Then dark hair fills my head, sending my thoughts elsewhere.

Green eyes haunt me. The flecks of gold are deeper in person, those plump lips trembling. The scent of coconut still lingers in the air. I shouldn't have touched her, held her so close.

The soft feel of her olive skin as her body pressed against mine sparked something to life inside me—something I thought was dead. And I need to shut that shit down. It's not gonna happen. She's the enemy. Nothing more.

I lose track of time as I continue to beat the shit out of the bag. My body shakes from the endorphin rush, but I don't stop. It's either fight or fuck this shit out of my system, and the latter is not an option.

"Someone pissed you off," Axel taunts as he leans against the wall across from me. I shoot him a quick glance before going back to what I'm doing. Axel doesn't heed the warning in my glare. "You know there are only two things that help me work through my anger and one of them is a hell of a lot more fun than punching a bag."

I ignore him and keep focused on ridding myself of any excess energy that remains. I'm afraid if I speak, I'll say something else I can't take back.

Sweat drips down my back, fueling my motivation. The balls of my feet shift with each hit as I picture the faces of the fuckers who took my life and turned it into the shit show it is now. My fists clench with the need to inflict pain, to rip them apart piece by piece. To feel their blood dripping down my hands. To watch their eyes become empty as their souls are dragged to Hell.

The bag swings against the chain the harder I punch, the impact felt all the way down to my bones. Moisture builds underneath my wraps, but I keep going. A little blood is nothing.

"What did you say to piss him off, Ax?" Zane comes to stand next to Axel, who is still watching my every move.

"Nothing. I just suggested he fuck it out of his system instead of hitting this like a damn pussy."

This time I do stop. Axel's turned into a cocky bastard since I've been away and I need to knock him down a peg or five. "Why don't you put your money where your mouth is?"

That shuts his ass up.

Zane tilts his head in Axel's direction and calls him out. "Yeah, man. Show us you still remember everything our ol' man taught us. Or are you just all talk and no action, little brother?"

Axel thinks about it for a bit and when he flashes me a shit-eating grin, I know I have him. "Fine." He pushes off the wall and walks over to slip on his gloves before he comes to stand in front of me. "You're not wearing any gloves?"

"Gloves are for pussies." I hold up my hands, giving him a direct view of my blood-soaked wraps.

"Fuck." Axel's eyes fix on them. He does his best to keep his face blank, but it's too late. I see the slight hesitation behind his gaze. That's all I need to give me the upper hand.

"A hundred bucks says he knocks you on your ass within the first five minutes." Zane pulls out a stool and makes himself comfortable.

"Seriously?" Axel whips his head toward Zane.

"Look at him." Zane shrugs. "He's the size of a fucking tank."

Axel shakes his head but doesn't back out. He can't. If he does, we'll never let him live it down. He brings his hands up in front of his face, waiting on me to make my move. "No face shots. I have a date later this week."

"No promises."

We bounce on the balls of our feet, keeping our steps light as we focus on each other. My fist aims for the side of his head, but he blocks it with his left one and swings a jab at me with his right. I'm able to block the hit with my arms before he can get me in the gut.

Round and round we go, each of us bobbing and weaving, dodging the others' fists. Axel is holding out better than I thought he would. I'm impressed with his ability to hold his own, but he's getting tired. The hits are becoming wide and sloppy. His endurance is no match for mine.

He throws a punch and drops his other hand a bit, exposing the left side of his face. I take advantage and nail him in the eye.

"Shit." He shakes it off but doesn't tap out.

His temper gets the best of him and starts coming at me fast and hard. I let him get a hit in and he's so focused on his victory that he doesn't see my fist until it's too late. I throw an uppercut, hitting Axel right under the chin. He's knocked down onto the mat and flat on his back.

"Fuck, man. What the hell was that?" Axel groans from his sprawled out position on the mat.

"That was what happens when you get cocky and let your guard down. Remember that because there are no second chances if you fuck up out there." I hold out my hand and help him sit up. His bottom lip is split open and there's a small cut along his right eyebrow, but other than that he's fine.

We sit and catch our breath while Zane watches from his seat. He knows I needed this. The longer he stares, the more my agitation grows. I hated the way I was always watched in prison, like I was some animal they might need to tase, and I'll be damned if one of my own does it to me.

"You know I hate it when you fucking stare like that. If you have something to say, just come out and say it." I don't spare him a glance as I unwrap my hands.

"All right." Zane laughs. "Now that we have her, what's our next move?"

I stop what I'm doing and meet his gaze head-on. "Now, we're gonna take them out one by one."

"Starting with that fucker, Benny?" Axel asks, looking ready to maim something.

"Tomorrow night." I nod.

"And Diego? He's bound to know she's missing by now." Zane presses his lips together into a firm line.

"We'll make the call in another day or so. Let him tear the city apart looking for her first."

"And the girl?" Axel dabs at his lip and glances up at me. He's too interested in Charlee and it's setting me on edge.

I wipe the blood off my knuckles, letting my silence speak for itself. Charlee's mine and I'll take my time with her.

CHAPTER TEN

ASHER

B ENNY ROLLS THE CREEPER UNDERNEATH a Corvette and goes to work, completely unaware that he's being watched. His radio is blaring Johnny Cash's "God's Gonna Cut You Down," making him both deaf and blind to his surroundings. *Idiot.* He'd never last a day in prison.

Our feet never make a sound as we enter the shop. I stop a few feet away from the passenger side of the Corvette, while Axel follows Zane toward the lift's control switch with his aluminum bat in his hand. I tilt my chin over the roof of the car and give Zane the signal. He pushes the release lever and the lift drops. Benny only manages to get his top half out from underneath the car before he's pinned down. He pushes against the car, but it's pointless. He ain't going nowhere. His groans of pain echo against the metal walls and my body lights up like the Fourth of July. Time for this piece of shit to pay his dues.

"You didn't secure your lift. That's not very smart, Benny." I cock my head to the side and glance down at him.

He's disoriented and struggling to make sense of things, but then his black beady eyes take me in, and I see the exact moment recognition flares behind them. "Detective Savage?"

My body tenses. I haven't heard that name in years and it's like pouring acid on an open wound. Something inside of me itches to break free, but I ignore the war that's battling underneath my skin and focus on him. "It's just Savage now."

And he's about to realize just how relevant that is.

"I thought you were locked up?" His dark eyebrows pinch together.

"He got out." Zane comes to stand next to me and crosses his arms over his chest.

Benny's Adam's apple bobs up and down as he takes in the sight of my brothers and me. We're scary as fuck on a good day, so I can only imagine what must be going through that small brain of his. He tries to put up a brave front, but I can see right through his bullshit. He's scared shitless and he should be.

"What do you want?" His voice cracks at the end of his question.

My eyes never leave his as I light up a cigarette. Benny flinches at the sound of my lighter clicking shut. That slight movement gives me the upper hand and only makes what I'm about to do that much sweeter.

I take a long, slow drag, letting my silence work him over. It's in those quiet moments when you can really mess with a person's head. Fear is the ultimate mind fuck. Leave them wondering, anticipating every possible outcome. Then, when they've tortured themselves to the brink of insanity, the fun really begins.

I exhale a cloud of smoke toward his face and let the silence linger a beat longer before I walk over and drop a photo on Benny's chest. "Names. I want all of them."

Axel watches from off to the side, keeping the bat cocked over his right shoulder. His fingers twitch against the handle as he paces back and forth. He's wound up tight and ready to go, but he waits for my lead.

"I don't know what you're talking about. Everything's legit here, man. I'm just a mechanic." He grins, but it doesn't reach his eyes. Piece of shit's holding out on me.

"You're a lousy liar, Benny. Maybe you need some motivation to jog your memory?" I give a silent nod to Axel.

"Batter up." He grins as he takes the bat in his hands and swings out in front of him like he's Babe Ruth. The first hit shatters the radio, blanketing us in silence, before he moves over toward the Corvette. Glass shatters and rains down on Benny in small shards. He does his best to protect his face, but he still manages to get some small scrapes along his arms.

Axel has a shit-eating grin on his face as he slings the bat over his shoulder once again. "I don't know about y'all, but I think that was a home run."

"Next swing my brother takes is aimed at your head." There's no mistaking the threat in my words.

"You're crazy." A muscle jumps on Benny's cheek.

"As a motherfucker." My eyes narrow as they lock on his.

"What the hell?" Benny squirms, but he's not going anywhere. "You can't do this."

"We can." Axel nudges him in the side with the tip of the bat.

"We are." Zane stares Benny down.

"I'm the judge, jury, and executioner. Now, tell me what I want to know. Or I'll let my brother use that bat on that shit hole you call a face."

"I can't tell you what I don't know." He's holding out longer than I thought he would. I'll give him that, but time's up. No more screwing around.

"You're full of shit. I know you're working for Diego." I flick the ash of my cigarette onto his chest and squat down until I'm inches from his face.

Benny flinches at the mention of Diego. It's slight, but there's no mistaking what I saw.

Zane moves so fast I almost miss it. One second he's next to me, and the next he has the sole of his boot pressed down on Benny's throat. Benny gasps as his oxygen supply is cut off. His hands slap against the tip of Zane's foot, struggling to breathe, causing the photo to fall off his chest and onto the shop floor.

I cock my head to the side and watch as the life starts to fade from his eyes. For a split second, I contemplate letting my brother finish him off, but that would leave us back at square one.

"Is he supposed to turn that shade of purple?" Axel asks, without a hint of concern. He might as well be asking about the weather.

Just when it looks like Benny's about to pass out, I tap my brother on the shoulder. "Ease up a bit, Z. He can't tell us anything if he's dead."

Zane relieves some of his pressure but doesn't take his foot away from Benny's neck. He's thirsting to feel bones break underneath his boot and as much as I agree with him on that, we need Benny alive a bit longer.

Benny coughs and sucks in gulps of air like a starving animal, but I don't give him a chance to recover. Time is everything and I don't have any to waste.

I grab the photo off the dirty floor and dust it off before I shove it back in his face. "I need names, Benny. Now!"

"I can't. They'll kill me, man." He whines like the pussy he is, but he'll get no sympathy from me. I lost that emotion the night I lost Lauren.

"What the fuck you think we're gonna do to you?" My patience is wearing thin. I'm tired of playing around with him. It's time for more drastic measures. I motion toward Axel.

"On it," he calls from behind my back. He grabs one of the cans of gasoline and hands Zane the other one. Axel starts dousing the entire shop in it, while Zane pours his on Benny.

Benny shakes his head from side to side and spits out the liquid that made its way into his mouth. "Wait! I'll talk. I'll talk, man."

"Names. I won't repeat myself again."

"Mateo and the one with the scar is his cousin Louis." The second the names are out of his mouth, my heart races. Finally, after all this time, I have the names of the bastards responsible.

"And where can we find *Mateo* and *Luis*?"

"I don't know. They're not the ones I usually deal with. They mostly do grunt work and shit."

"You must have heard something in passing conversation. Think, Benny!"

His body shivers as he wracks his small brain for any piece of information that I can use. "They hang out at the strip club over on Main and Tenth."

"Which one?" Zane presses his foot down once more.

"Viper's Den! It's called Viper's Den."

"Was that so hard?" I pat the side of his face and get to my feet. Without a word, my brothers follow me out of the shop. We got what we came for. No need to waste another breath on this asshole. At the edge of the bay door, I stop and turn back around. I take one last drag before tossing the lit butt of my cigarette onto the puddle of gasoline near Benny's head and lifting the corner of my mouth in a half-ass grin.

"What the hell, man?" He struggles to break free from the car, but it's no use. He's a sitting duck who's about to be fucked. Flames ignite right next to him and in a matter of seconds, he's on fire as well. "No!"

"Bye, Benny." I turn and follow my brothers the rest of the way to the truck. Once we reach it, Zane tosses the gas cans in the bed and leans against the tailgate.

"Am I missing something?" Axel scratches the side of his head with the tip of the bat. "I thought the whole point of this was to send Diego a message?"

Zane is wearing the same uncertain expression on his face. I stare back at both of my brothers, keeping my own face blank. They should know me better by now. I give nothing away.

Axel opens his mouth to say something else, but his words are cut off by a loud boom. The shop explodes, engulfed in a ball of flames.

"Message sent." I arch an eyebrow at my brothers, letting my point sink in.

Axel shakes his head and laughs. "Crazy motherfucker."

This crazy motherfucker's just getting started.

CHAPTER
ELEVEN

CHARLEE

THERE'S A HEAVY WEIGHT OF foreboding crushing down on my chest as I lie there on the hard mattress. My eyes are dry and puffy, and I feel the beginning of a headache stirring. The skin around my throat is sore and tender from his viselike grip. Every limb in my body aches from the shivers that have racked my body all night long. I swear the air conditioning was left on just to add more discomfort to my new accommodations.

Curling into a ball, I burrow under the thin blanket, seeking any warmth I can find, but it's pointless. Cold still manages to seep into my bones. I need my damn clothes back. It doesn't help matters that the sleep I did manage to get came in short, restless bursts.

Meanwhile, sunlight beats down from the large window, illuminating my prison. It makes the space look warm and inviting—a total lie. I keep the blanket wrapped around my body and push up to a sitting position. I take in more of my surroundings, hoping that things have changed, that the past two nights were somehow a bad dream, but no such luck.

"You're royally screwed, Charlee," I whisper to myself.

The sound of a lock turning causes my spine to stiffen. My head whips up and I brace to face my unknown fate head-on. His massive form fills the doorway, blocking out everything else. A light gray t-shirt hugs his broad shoulders, drawing attention to every hard ridge of muscle underneath. Khaki green cargo pants are loosely tucked into his tan work boots.

A five o'clock shadow covers the rough edges of his square jaw and has my heart pounding against my chest. Whether the increase in blood flow is from fear or something else, something I refuse to acknowledge, I'm not entirely sure. There's no denying he's attractive, but most monsters are.

There's a tray of food in his large hands. I've been so absorbed in taking in his appearance that it escaped my attention until now. I lick my lips at the steaming plate. It's been too long since I've eaten, but while my stomach growls, I won't touch a single bite. I'd rather die than take what he's offering. Who knows what he's done to it?

When his blue eyes lock on mine, a shudder courses through me. They're still as cold and lifeless as I remember. Then his gaze travels to my neck and lingers there. My hand comes up to trace the tender skin as his nostrils flare. I haven't looked, but I can already feel the bruises forming.

A muscle jumps in his cheek, but other than that I have no idea what he's thinking. The hard lines of his face remain stoic and give nothing away.

My eyes dart back down to the tray of food and I gnaw on my bottom lip to keep from breaking.

"It's not poisoned." A corner of his mouth lifts in a smile that never reaches his eyes as he steps into the room.

"And I'm just supposed to believe you?" I snort and wave a hand in his direction. The slight movement causes the blanket to slip off my shoulder, exposing my bra. Every muscle in his body goes rigid, but his eyes remain the same stormy shade of blue. Other than the clenching of his jaw, there's no indication that this man is affected by me or that he feels anything at all for that matter.

After a beat of tense silence, he shakes his head and enters the room the rest of the way, reaching the bed in a few large strides. I grip the itchy material of the thin blanket tighter in my fists the closer he gets. My body's moving into flight or fight mode. I stay focused on his every move, waiting for an opportunity. I'm like a cat with my claws out, ready to spring up and attack at the first chance at freedom.

He sets the tray down on the nightstand next to the bed and steps back. I do a quick glance, inspecting its contents, and disappointment hits. He hasn't given me anything I can use as a weapon. There are no utensils of any kind, the water is in a plastic cup, and even the food is on a paper plate.

"You really think I'd make it that easy for you?" His dark voice taunts me.

My eyebrows pinch together as I glare up at him. I was hoping he would.

"Eat," he barks out like I'm a damn dog, expected to follow his command.

I jump at the sharp edge in his tone but make no effort to answer him otherwise. If he wants me to cooperate, he'll have to ask me nicely.

"I won't tell you again." There's no missing the warning in his voice, but too bad for him, I've never been a good listener.

"I'm not hungry." My voice comes out in a low rasp.

We have another brief stand-off, but this time he gives in first.

"Fine. Suit yourself." He turns to walk away, dismissing me, and my blood boils. All common sense leaves me. It's the only explanation for what happens. The tray is out of my hands before I've even realized it, and it nails him dead center in the middle of his back. I don't even remember jumping to my feet or grabbing the tray.

Scrambled egg and toast fall onto the wooden floor in a limp heap. Water from my cup splashes against his back, soaking his gray shirt.

He stops mid-step and spins on his heel, stalking toward me. Judging by his clenched jaw, I've just royally screwed up. I move, running past him in the direction of the open doorway, but trip over my own feet. The hardness of the floor hits my ass, knocking the wind out of me. I flip over and continue crawling to the door, not caring that the material of my thong is digging into my ass crack and giving him one hell of a view.

The sound of his boots stomping against the floor behind me has my pulse racing. I'm not sure what he's going to do if he catches me and I have no intention of finding out.

I'm just past the doorway when I'm grabbed from behind and shoved against a rock hard chest. A hand fists my hair while the other wraps around my chest. My head is jerked back so far that the muscles of my sore neck strain.

"That wasn't very nice," he grunts against my ear, the heat of his body causing shivers to race through mine.

"Let me go." I thrash against him like a wild animal.

"Not until you learn." His deep voice vibrates against my back.

"Fuck you!" My fingers dig into the flesh of his hands, catching bits of skin underneath my nails. I keep fighting until I feel the wetness of his blood dripping down his hands.

"Keep going." He laughs and walks us back into the room. "I like the pain. It reminds me that I'm still alive."

Things happen so fast. One minute I'm pressed against his chest and the next I'm being thrust forward and forced down onto all fours like I'm the damn dog he thinks me to be.

"Eat." His demand causes fire to churn in the pit of my stomach.

I brace my arms on the floor and dig my hands into the wood. My body pushes back against his force with everything I have, but it's useless. He's too strong.

"Lesson number one, Charlee. You act like an animal and I'll treat you like one." He shoves my head down until the wetness of the scrambled egg is pushed up against my nose and mouth, smothering me. "Now open up and eat your breakfast like a good little girl."

I hold my breath and keep my mouth tightly closed as long as I can. One small breath and I'll inhale nothing but egg. Seconds tick by and soon my vision begins to blacken. I have no other choice. Either I do as he asks or I'm going to suffocate. On a whimper, my lips part and allow the yellow pile of mush inside my mouth. I let it sit on my tongue, but make no motion to swallow it. I'll spit in the trash when this asshole leaves.

"Swallow." His grip tightens, the pressure causing pain to radiate over my scalp. I do as he commands and choke back my anger. "Now say 'thank you.'"

"Go to hell!" I spit back and struggle against his hold. The hardwood floor digs into my kneecaps, but I suck it up and ignore the bite of pain.

He lets out another laugh that sounds forced. "You have no idea what Hell is, but you're about to, Princess." With that, he releases me and stomps off. My fingers curl into fists as I sit on my butt and watch him walk away. At the doorway, he pauses and looks over his shoulder at me. "Your father did you no favors by sheltering you."

I flinch at the sound of the door slamming and then the dam of emotions I've been holding in breaks. I grab the tray off the floor and throw it at the door.

"I fucking hate you!" Tears brim, soaking my bottom lashes, and I let them fall. He may have won this battle, but I'll win the war. This isn't over by a long shot. I'm not done fighting. Even if it takes my last breath, I will get out of this fucking prison.

CHAPTER
TWLEVE

CHARLEE

I'M NOT SURE HOW LONG I sit on the floor with my knees hugged up against my chest, but it's long enough that the bits of egg have dried on my face and in my hair. I should move and sit on the bed, but the coldness of the floor is the only thing keeping me awake. I hate feeling so dirty, so unclean, and a part of me thinks my captor enjoys watching me suffer like this, taking great joy in the fact that he's tarnished the great Diego Vega's daughter.

Little does he know, I'm no spoiled little dove who's spent her life locked inside a gilded cage left to wither away. My father knew I'd need to survive on my own in the cruel world he runs, and he prepared me for situations such as this.

The moment I hear the latch of the lock being twisted, my body stiffens. My captor steps into the room, leaving the door open behind him. His face is blank, empty of any emotion. Those cold, dead eyes meet mine and I hold his gaze. I know he probably expects me to look away, to cower in fear, but I won't give him the satisfaction.

After our last encounter I need to tread carefully, so I don't run off at the mouth just yet. One wrong move and he'll snap. I need to keep him talking, distract him enough to let his guard down, and the moment his back is turned, run like hell.

"Go shower and put these on." He tosses a t-shirt that smells an awful lot like him at me, along with a pair of white lace underwear and a matching bra that still have the tags attached. I should be alarmed that they're both in my size and something I'd pick out for myself, but this man seems like he's planned everything out, right to the very last detail. Like he's spent a good amount of time studying me, watching me without my knowledge. The thought sends shivers up my spine.

"Don't make me repeat myself, Charlee. You'll regret it." He crosses his arms in front of him, causing his shirt to stretch over the mountain of muscle that is his chest as he watches me.

When I make no move to do as he demands, he reaches out and grips me by the arm. In one fell swoop, I'm tossed over his shoulder like I weigh next to nothing. He stomps toward the tiny bathroom with my hands slapping his back. He slides me down his body to my feet and points a tattooed finger at me.

"Stay." He twists to turn the shower on, expecting me to listen to his command like I'm a pet he can order around. He's sadly mistaken on that. I take advantage and shove him forward directly into the spray of water. His gargled shouts don't deter me one bit as I spin on the balls of my feet and run in the direction of the open door like I'm on fire.

This time I do make it through the doorway, but that's as far as I get. A massive body comes from out of nowhere and I slam right into a hard wall of muscle. I glance up to find a similar pair of blue eyes staring down at me, but these ones aren't as cold. They hold a bit of humor in them as they look down at me. The more I take in his appearance, the more I realize the similarities. Both he and my captor have the same build and tanned skin. There's no missing the family resemblance. There are minor differences of course. A few tattoos are on display on the side of just one arm. He also has a full beard and a messy man bun on top of his head.

He glances over my shoulder and directs his attention to my

captor, cutting off my gawking. "She giving you problems, Asher?" And now I have a name to go with the bastard behind me.

"Nope. I've got her, Zane." A wet hand clamps down on my upper arm, yanking me back against a rock-hard chest. His other arm comes around my front, pinning me in place. Wetness from his shirt soaks my naked back the tighter his hold becomes, but I make no complaint. Not that it would matter if I did. He'd ignore it like he does everything else in regards to me. I swear this man must have a heart of ice.

Zane spares us one last glance before his hard eyes land on mine. "All right then. I'll leave you to it." With that, he walks away, leaving me alone with the jerk face behind me.

Asher moves to turn us around, but I don't cooperate. I'm not going to make anything easy for him. My body wriggles against his grip, squirming and kicking like a wild animal. It's enough to knock him off balance, causing him to stumble a bit. It doesn't make him lose his hold on me, which just pisses me off.

"Lesson number two, Princess. Don't piss me off. You won't like what I do to you if you do." His lips brush against the shell of my ear as he whispers against my neck. The short hairs of his stubble scrape against the side of my cheek and I shiver with every word he utters.

He forces us back into the room and toward the bathroom. "We need to clean you up before we call *Daddy*."

I don't have time for his words to fully register before I'm airborne and dumped on my ass inside the shower. Cold water hits my body the second he tosses me inside like I'm a dead weight. I scream and fight against the onslaught of ice that's penetrating me down to my bones, but he holds me down under the spray. Water burns down my nostrils as I choke on a mouthful of it, gasping for air.

"That's fucking cold, you bastard," I spit out as I scratch and claw at any part of him I can reach. It does nothing to stop him, though.

When I open my eyes, he's much closer than I expected, and I can make out even more detail on his face. He has a few scars hidden underneath a skull tattoo on his neck. My hand reaches up to touch the intricate images, making contact with the warm skin of his neck, and he flinches at the sudden contact. It's slight, but it's there.

Water drips down his dark lashes, down his face and onto the collar of his shirt as his blue eyes deepen and we're locked in a stare. This time I don't find the hardness I usually do. There's something else, something that looks an awful lot like warmth brewing behind them, but before I can make head or tale of it, the wall is slammed back into place and I'm left staring at the heartless bastard I've come to hate.

"Sorry, we don't have amenities to your liking, Princess. But this isn't a fucking hotel. I won't cater to your spoiled ass. The sooner you learn that, the better."

"Fuck you!" My hands slap against the wet tile, causing water to splash out onto the floor.

"No way in hell would I ever stoop so low." He lets out a fake laugh. "Get cleaned up. You have ten minutes and if you're not ready, then I'm coming in to do it myself."

"I hope my father chops your balls off and crams them down your throat when he finds you," I yell to his retreating back. He stops in the doorway, clenching and unclenching his fists. I should probably stop baiting him, but I've never been very good at shutting my mouth and being somebody's doormat. This bastard is sadly mistaken if he thinks for one minute that I'm going to behave like a good little toy and do whatever I'm told. I'm Charlee motherfucking Vega and I will bow to no one.

CHAPTER
THIRTEEN

ASHER

A TRAIL OF WATER FOLLOWS me across the hall as I leave her to finish up in the shower. I go straight into my room, not stopping until I'm in my bathroom. It's all white from top to bottom inside. There's not a trace of color anywhere, but I like it this way. It's clean of any stains from my past, and it's all mine. A sharp contrast to the ones I had to use in prison with several others at the same time. Privacy isn't something I'll take for granted ever again.

I pull off my shirt and toss it on the floor. I'll pick it up later. I have more important things to do right now. Grabbing a towel off the rack, I start wiping at the water droplets that cover my neck and chest. My temper's so far gone that I don't realize how much pressure I'm using until I feel the burning of my skin. I throw it next to my shirt and grip the sides of the sink. My head hangs as I struggle to keep my breathing even. Every time I deal with her, she throws me for a fucking loop, does the opposite of what I expect her to. Not to mention I fucking flinched at the heat of her touch. It felt like fire branding into my skin. It's both aggravating and intriguing all at the same time, and that just pisses me off.

Goddamn her!

I exhale another long breath and struggle to get my pulse under control. If I don't get my shit together, I may end up wringing her neck. The damn dark-haired vixen is nothing like I thought she'd be. She's fire and ice all wrapped up in one tiny little body.

Movement out of the corner of my eye catches my attention and I know who it is before he even speaks. His footsteps are much heavier than Zane's.

"You okay there, big brother? Z said you had a little bit of trouble with your hellcat." There's no missing the humor in Axel's voice. The fucker's enjoying watching me come unhinged more than he should.

"Not now, Ax." I don't have it in me to put up with his shit right now.

To my relief, he listens and doesn't say anything else. He leans against the doorjamb and watches me lose my shit over a woman half my size. She may be a tiny thing, but fuck me if her temper isn't as large as mine.

"She's so fucking stubborn." I meet his eyes through the reflection in the mirror and sigh.

"Sounds like someone else I know." His mouth curves into a wide smile like my frustrations are the funniest thing he's ever seen.

"The fuck if it does. I am not anything like her." Despite what he thinks, he's wrong. To compare us is like comparing oil to water. We're nothing alike.

"Right." Axel doesn't look convinced one fucking bit and it grates on my nerves.

I ignore the feeling that's settling into my bones at what he's implying and walk past him to grab a dry shirt from my closet. The first one I find I throw on. It doesn't matter that it happens to be a dark shade of green or that it matches the color of her eyes perfectly. That's just a coincidence.

Turning my back on Axel's laughing ass, I make my way back to the little demon. I don't need to look at the time to know her ten minutes are up and if they aren't, oh fucking well.

I'm shocked as shit when I walk in to find that she's done exactly as I've asked. She's showered and dressed in one of my t-shirts, glaring at me. The shirt's so big it hits her just above her knees. Her dark hair is sopping wet and clings to the sides of her face—a face that's now free of makeup and showing off a perfect olive complexion.

Blood flows south, making my jeans uncomfortably tight. There's just something about seeing her in my clothes that has my dick springing to life. I fight against the ache in my pants and focus on the raven-haired vixen in front of me. She's the enemy. I need to remember that or things are going to get fucked before I've even started.

The points of her nipples poke against the thin cotton material, no doubt remnants of the cold shower she endured. It's enough to almost make me feel like the bastard she believes me to be—almost. If she'd just fucking cooperate and do as I say she'd realize things wouldn't always be this difficult. Then she glances behind me and her calm demeanor flies out the window.

"You!" Like a wild banshee, she charges for my brother. Her tiny hands ball into fists as she punches against his chest. "If you hurt Kelsey, I'm going to cut your balls off."

I should probably stop her, but I'm enjoying the fact that her rage is aimed at someone else for the moment. Plus, I'm still annoyed with Axel's earlier comment, so this is what he gets—a little payback for busting my balls.

"Whoa there, Hellcat." Axel raises his hands in mock surrender. He keeps them up and doesn't make a move to stop her, which is good because if he puts his hands on her, I may lose my shit. "She's safe at home."

"Bullshit," Charlee snaps as she continues to hit him. I should probably stop her, and I might…eventually.

"It's the truth. I swear on Willie Mae that she's fine." Axel's voice has gone soft as if he's talking down a wild animal, and I guess the comparison isn't that far off. Charlee is proving to be a bit feral.

She stops her assault and stares at him like he's lost his mind, which is a strong possibility. "Who?"

"His truck," I offer up from behind them, causing her attention to shift back to me.

"And that's supposed to mean something to me?" She puts her hands on her hips, causing the hem of my t-shirt to ride higher up her thighs, and glares at me. The movement is small, but her attitude is large as fuck. It's an image that has my dick straining against the zipper of my jeans in appreciation.

"He loves that truck more than anything. So, if he swears on that, Princess, then he's dead serious." I fight to gain control and keep my shit together while I answer her.

"I am." A muscle jerks in Axel's cheek as he answers her.

"Let's go." Situation handled, I grab her arm and lead her out into the hall. I'll get what crawled up his ass out of Axel later. We have enough shit going on right now without adding more to the pile.

A faint scent of lemons hits me, and I do my best to ignore the way the scent of my shampoo smells better coming off of Charlee or the way her soft skin feels under my hand as we descend the stairs.

Axel must catch something on my face because he just grins and gives me a knowing look. I shake it off and keep walking.

When we walk into the basement, Zane is ready and waiting for us. Charlee's back goes ramrod straight the minute she sees the lone chair in the center of the room. I didn't need to drag her all the way down here to make the call, but I knew it would throw her off if I did. Messing with her has become one of my favorite pastimes. If I focus all my hate, all my rage on her, it keeps the nightmares and all the other shit inside my head at bay and that's enough for me for now.

"Sit." A part of me feels like a sack of shit for ordering her around so much, but the more she's scared of me, the better my plans will work.

She hesitates for a brief second before sitting in the chair. Her body scoots back until it's flush with the backrest, causing her feet to dangle off the floor a bit as her wide eyes take everything in. She's assessing, scheming to come up with an escape route. She thinks I don't notice what she's doing, but she's wrong. The determined look in her eyes is one I'm all too familiar with. She's Diego's daughter through and through.

Axel hands me the rope off the floor and I get to work tying her up at her wrists and ankles.

"Seriously?" She arches a dark eyebrow at me as her plump lips purse together. There's a fire behind her gaze, driving home the same burning need in mine. This is going to be a battle of wills, and I will come out on top.

"Yes, Princess. Get over it." I grind my teeth to keep my cool. That fucking mouth of hers is going to be the death of me. I'm quick and efficient with my knots and have her all tied up in less than a minute. I tug on the ropes for one last test before I walk over to the laptop I had Axel bring down earlier and set it up for a video call.

"Yes." He answers on the first ring. His suit is wrinkled and his hair's a mess. There's no trace of the put together criminal I've come to know. He's been waiting for this call. Behind him is Marco.

"Been a long time, Diego, huh?" My fingers dig into the sides of the monitor. Seeing the turmoil on his face is the only thing keeping me calm.

"Let me talk to my daughter, Savage." Guess we're not going to do the bullshit routine of small talk; that's fine with me.

"I'll do you one better." I twist the laptop around, giving him a full view of Charlee's sitting form. "There she is."

"You okay, *Mija*?" Hearing the softer tone he takes with her, as a parent would with their child, annoys the shit out of me. I could have had that, but he robbed me of that privilege.

"I'm fine, *Papá*." Her voice comes out smooth and controlled. A momentary sense of admiration washes over me. She's keeping her shit together much better than I thought she would.

I spin the computer back around to face me. "You get my present? It's too bad Benny wasn't more careful."

His dark eyebrows narrow at my words, and in that slight mannerism, I see a small resemblance to Charlee, but that's where the similarities end. She inherited her olive skin and green eyes from her mother.

"You're fucking dead, *Puto!*" Marco slams his fist down on the desk so hard the monitor rattles.

"What do you want?" Diego puts a hand out to shut him up and turns his attention back to me. There's no missing the dark circles under his eyes. He probably hasn't slept much since he discovered Charlee missing. *Good.* Let him sweat and wonder how I'm violating his princess.

"You know what I want." The fact that he's playing stupid right now only adds fuel to my fire.

"You want money? Is that it?" He leans against his desk and closer to the screen. "Let my daughter go and we'll talk. Settle this like men."

A dark laugh escapes me at his use of the word 'men.' "Oh, I'm gonna settle this all right. You took from me and now I'm gonna take from you."

His throat bobs up and down as he swallows, and that's the only hint I get that he's even pissed at me taking his precious little girl. "If you lay a finger on her I'm going to—"

I force out a small smile at the torment written on this bastard's face. I have what he loves most at my fingertips and it's killing him. "Going to what? Kill me? Torture me? Nothing you can do to me is any worse than what I've suffered, what I've lost, so bring it on, motherfucker."

"You son of a bitch! I'm going to—"

"We'll be in touch." I end the call, but not before I hear him and Marco let out another string of curses. Good to know I've struck a nerve. Phase one is complete. It's time for phase two.

CHAPTER
FOURTEEN

CHARLEE

A FTER ASHER HUNG UP WITH my dad, he and the other two, who I've come to realize are his brothers, have been talking in code. I don't understand much, but from what little I can gather, I was right. They have it out for my dad and I'm just collateral damage caught in the crossfire.

It took another ten minutes of arguing before Asher finally untied me and led me back to my room. Without a word, he shoved me through and locked me inside. Now, I'm sitting here with nothing to do but plot my escape.

That phone call was torture. It took everything I had to keep myself together. I didn't like seeing the worry on my father's face. Despite our disagreements, he's always been my protector. We may not see eye to eye on many things and I might not want anything to do with his lifestyle, but that doesn't mean I'm heartless.

A sigh escapes me as I glance around my prison. I wish I had some of my drawing supplies. Sketching would help pass the time while I'm stuck in here, but I'll survive. Asher can keep me locked up, but he'll never dampen my spirits.

My fingers toy with the hem of the t-shirt I'm wearing. Taking a cold shower was torture, but washing away the past couple of days was like washing away some of my sins. Whiskey and tobacco are embedded deep into the fabric. Figures. Even in his absence, I'm surrounded by him.

When he returns, he has a tray of food and a blue blanket tucked under his arm. He tosses the blanket onto the foot of the bed and then sets the tray of food down in front of me.

My hands make no move to reach for either item. Instead, I stare at the bundle of soft material like it's a foreign object. This is the same man who threw me in an ice cold shower over an hour ago, and now it's like a switch has been flipped. It leaves me wondering what his game is.

"I told you. If you're good, you get rewarded. And Princess, you were, so that's yours." His chin dips toward the blue blanket.

"Right." I nod, but still keep my hands in my lap. There's no telling what mood he's in and if I'm getting out of here, I need to be patient. I'll bide my time until I can catch him off guard and that's when I'll strike.

"Eat," he orders, but his voice isn't as harsh as I've become used to.

I should do as he says, but I don't trust him. Instead, I watch him like a hawk. He's doing the same through narrowed eyes. A part of me wonders what's going through his head, what's happened to make him like this. Another part doesn't care to figure out the psyche of a madman.

My stomach chooses this moment to growl so loud that I'm sure he's heard it from his position across the room. The smug grin that appears only confirms it.

"I know you're hungry, Princess. No need for niceties. You want to dig into your lunch then have at it. Nothing's stopping you."

Hunger takes over all sense and I shovel a decent sized piece in my mouth. It's been so long since I've eaten that I'm famished. The bread and turkey feel like a five-course meal on my tongue. There's no stopping the groan that slips out as I devour it.

Asher watches me, fascination etched on his face. The sudden attention has me shifting against the lumpy mattress.

"Why are you being nice to me?" I ask between bites.

"I told you, Charlee. You follow the rules and things will go much easier for you." His eyes narrow at me.

The piece of bread I'm swallowing sticks in my throat, making me gasp for air at his words. I don't even know Asher's moved until he's in front of me.

"Here. Drink this. It should help but take small sips so you don't choke more." He kneels down in front of me with a cup of water in his outstretched hand.

I take it from him and do as he suggests. When the choking finally subsides, I watch him for a few beats. He's an enigma. A puzzle. One I can't decide if I want to figure out or not.

"What has my father done for you to kidnap me?"

He ignores me and gets to his feet. If he thinks his silence will deter me, he's dead wrong. I'm not one to give up easily.

I keep at him, hoping my prying will cause him to slip. When he continues to keep quiet, I lose my shit. I jump to my feet and get in his space. "Know what I think? I think you're a coward."

"You don't know what the fuck you're talking about." The muscles in his throat flex and I know I've hit a nerve.

"I'm right, aren't I? You're nothing but a fucking coward. I mean, you kidnapped me and didn't even ask for any money." I kept my cool during the phone call, but all bets are off now.

"Be quiet, Princess, or I'll make you." His breathing becomes more erratic the closer into his space I get, and I should take that as the warning it is, but I'm too far gone to care about his warnings. As far as I'm concerned, he can shove them up his ass.

"Fuck you! I'm not some little kid you can just order around." The tip of my finger digs into the enormous wall of muscle, otherwise known as his chest, emphasizing my words and causing his whole body to stiffen.

"Last warning, Charlee." The words leave him in a low guttural tone, and again, I ignore the signs that I should stop.

The vein on the side of my neck throbs as my temper gets the best of me. "You don't have the balls to confront my father like a man, so you pick on someone weaker than you. You're worse than a coward. You're a—"

"I warned you, Princess." A hand whips out and grabs me by the back of the head as his other digs into my waist, cutting off my words with his lips.

A gasp of shock escapes me at the sudden movement, and he takes full advantage. Traces of whiskey and tobacco fill my mouth as his tongue thrusts inside, devouring me. My hands fist the cotton material of his shirt to keep from falling over as his mouth continues to work me into stunned silence. Those lips are methodical and demanding as they continue to dominate. To own me. They're warm and soft, a huge contrast to the cold, hard-ass in front of me.

His fingers thread through my hair, grabbing a fistful and pulling me in further, deepening the kiss. My lips move in tandem with his as our tongues clash together. Every push and pull of his lips has me following his lead, chasing for more.

Stubble from his five o'clock shadow scrapes against the sensitive skin of my cheeks as he continues to work me over with his mouth. His tongue flicks against mine and my body melts further into him. Warmth pools deep in my belly as my toes curl against the cold wood floor and I become lost in him.

When he breaks away, the heat of his body leaves mine and I don't like how empty I feel at the loss. My lips tingle, reeling from the aftershocks of his touch. His fingers linger on the nape of my neck, leaving a trail of heat behind them. "I'm getting something much better than money, Charlee."

His fingers tighten their hold on me as he pulls away just enough to whisper against my lips, "I've got you, and I'm going to use you to break him."

CHAPTER
FIFTEEN

ASHER

THE MINUTE THE WATER SHUTS off, I know something's up. It's gone quiet. Too fucking quiet. And all of the bodies next to me have disappeared. I wipe away the excess water and open my eyes to find three sets of brown eyes fixed on me.

I knew it was them. The stench of shit was thick in the air. These stupid fucks have been itching to get to me since I was locked up. They couldn't surprise me from behind because I learned from day one you never give them your back. It's a weakness they'll pounce on. So, like the sacks of shit they are, they waited until I was vulnerable.

"What do you want, Cyrus?" I clench my fists together as I force myself to keep calm. Fear is like a drug here. One hit and they'll keep coming at you for more until there's not a piece of you left.

"We have a little business to settle with you, Pig." He cocks his head to the side, in Viktor and Xander's direction. Both of them glare at me with busted lips and black eyes. I smile back at my handiwork. That'll teach them to try to jump me in the yard.

"Is that right?" Standing taller, I cross my arms over my chest. It's an intimidation tactic that's served me well in here so far.

"That's right." Xander steps forward, his fists hanging at his sides. Someone's a sore loser. That's what he gets for picking a fight with someone smarter than he is.

"It's an eye for an eye. You know how it works in here." Cyrus shrugs, but I can hear what he's not saying. It's more than business for him. This is personal. For whatever reason, he's taken an interest in me, and I need to squash that shit now.

"Your lip looks better." I flash Viktor a wide smile and enjoy watching him tense up. None of them can hide the fact that I'm getting under their skin.

Viktor grinds his teeth together. "That was a cheap shot, asshole."

"Right." I keep them talking as I think on the fly for a way out of here that doesn't end with a dick in my ass. "So was sucker punching me from behind like a little bitch."

"Shut up," Cyrus shouts at the two dip shits to be quiet and I know I'm standing on borrowed time before I'm fucked.

"Can you hurry it up and get to the point? You might get off standing there staring at my dick, but I can promise you the view ain't pretty from my end." My hand motions from my naked body to theirs. When they don't answer, I move to walk past them, but I'm cut off.

"Not so fast, pretty boy." Viktor steps in front of me, blocking my exit. Things are going to go downhill fast, so I need to use the element of surprise. I don't give him time to see what's happening before my fist is connecting with his face. We roll around on the cold cement, fighting for dominance. It doesn't matter that our dicks are probably flopping around; this is a fight to the death because I don't want any part of what they have planned for me.

I manage to gain the upper hand and crack him in the face again. Pain ricochets up my arm and I exhale at how good it feels. I clench my fist, ready to deliver the knockout punch, but this isn't boxing, and these fuckers fight dirty.

Xander comes at me from behind. All the air leaves me as he socks me in the side. At the same time, Viktor manages to get out from under me and nail me in the side of the head. I can feel the sting of split skin as blood drips down into my eye. They take advantage of this and grab me by the arms. I'm forced onto my knees with my head pulled back.

"As much shit as you talk, I thought you'd be packing more. Or was your *shower just real cold." I spit blood onto the floor near Cyrus' feet. That remark earns me another punch to the mouth, courtesy of Xander.*

"You've got a mouth on you. And I'm going to put it to good use." Cyrus' eyes go black as he licks his lips.

"You know what we do to pigs in here?" Xander laughs.

"We make them squeal," Viktor grunts in my ear.

"Fuck you, motherfucker." I fight against them, but I'm outnumbered and can't win. This is when things go from bad to worse.

"The only one who'll be fucked here is you, pig." Cyrus strokes his dick and licks his lips. "Open his mouth."

Viktor tightens his grip on my hair while Xander forces my mouth open. Acid builds in the back of my throat the closer Cyrus gets. I can't believe this shit is really going to happen to me.

I'm tangled in my sheets as I jerk awake. Beads of sweat cover my body and my heart pounds against my chest at a violent pace, but I'm safe. I'm not back there. I scrub a hand over my face and do my best to calm myself. These fucking nightmares are getting old. I left prison, but what good does being free do me if my own head's becoming one?

I grab a cigarette from the pack on the nightstand and light up. More memories fight their way in, but these are better ones. The looks on their faces when Carl knocked Cyrus out. Or when I beat the shit out of them once more. From that day forward things weren't better, but they weren't worse either. Carl saved my ass back there and we had each other's backs from then on.

There's no chance I'm falling back to sleep now, so I finish my cigarette and hop in the shower. Brown eyes are all I see when I close my eyes and let the heat of the water penetrate my aching body.

The eyes are always the first thing I notice on someone. They tell you everything you need to know. People can hide the fucked up shit in their minds or use their bodies to manipulate you, but it's the eyes that give them away every single time.

It doesn't matter if they're the dead brown ones that belong to a sick fuck like Cyrus or if they're the deepest shade of emerald and belong to a petite raven-haired princess.

Just the thought of the fire that resonates behind her eyes has my dick getting hard. It's been aching for release since the first time she taunted me with those plump, soft lips. Lips that I've tasted. She tasted of lemons and candy. The perfect mixture of sour and sweet has my mouth watering for more.

My dick begs for attention at the thought. I lean my left hand against the wall of the shower, wrap the fist of my right hand around my length, and squeeze. A mixture of pleasure and pain hits me all at once.

Water beats down on my back as I stroke myself from root to tip. Visions of Charlee, naked and on her knees in front of me, fill my head. I close my eyes, losing myself in the sight. It won't ever happen, but this is one hell of a fucking fantasy.

Her olive skin glistens with water as she grips me with her tiny hands and works me with a strong, steady pace. Hungry green eyes meet mine as the tip of my dick breaches her eager mouth. My ass muscles flex as I thrust the rest of the way inside. Everything is tight. Warm and wet. Her mouth is fucking perfect. The feel of her lips suctioning my dick has the base of my spine tingling. Her tongue moves, wiggling around my dick. The sensation is toxic and inviting all at the same time.

A groan escapes me as I toss my head back and enjoy every second I'm inside her. I'm so far gone that I can't last much longer. Not even digging my teeth into my bottom lip so hard I taste blood is enough to stop the hunger that's overpowering me. One last flick of her tongue has my balls drawing up tight against my body. A few more strokes are all it takes for my dick to twitch against my hand, spilling years' worth of cum onto my fingers.

For a brief moment, I'm left in a fog of numbness, enjoying the high of it all. My heart pounds against my chest as I let it wash over me. Then the reality of what I've just done crashes down on me like a lead weight.

A wave of sickness hits me and my fist slams into the cold tile. *What the fuck am I doing?* I'm losing it and I need to get a grip before I end up fucking her and fuck everything to shit.

CHAPTER
SIXTEEN

ASHER

A FTER WHAT HAPPENED IN THE shower, I needed space. I let Axel take the reins with Charlee so I could plan out what's going down tonight with a clear head. The fact that I was stuck at my desk and my attention would drift to her door every few minutes is irrelevant. Or at least that's the bullshit I tell myself. The past two days, I've been as jumpy as a fucking squirrel. My hands bounced on my leg with the need to fight or fuck, which is why we're here hunting at Viper's Den.

Sweat and cigarettes taint the air. It's almost overshadowed by the number of half-naked bodies that are writhing around. Lights flicker as "Wasp" by Motionless in White blares through the shitty sound system.

Naked women are everywhere. It's a buffet of tits and ass. Some are serving drinks to nearby tables in nothing but G-strings and pasties to cover their oversized tits. Another few are giving lap dances to what appear to be drunken frat boys. On the stage are a couple of naked dancers working the pole in nothing but black fuck-me heels.

"Hello, ladies." Axel's attention is glued to the pairs of fake tits up on stage. He's lost in the jiggling flesh like a horny pup that just learned how to use his dick for the first time.

"Focus, Dickhead." Zane smacks him on the back of the head, saving me the trouble.

"I was." Axel rubs the spot where he was just hit but doesn't take his eyes off the stage.

I scan the room and head to the first empty table I find. It's off to the corner but gives me a full view of the room.

A waitress wastes no time coming over to take our orders. "What can I get for y'all?" She adjusts the tray in her arms to the side and leans in. The musky stench of her perfume is enough to choke me. It's bitter and stale, nothing like the citrusy scent of Charlee. My fists clench as I do my damnedest not to lose focus thinking about her and those fuckable lips.

"Your number." Axel flashes her the same smile that used to work on our parents and get him out of shit as a kid.

"Ain't you funny." She laughs and shakes her head. At least she's smart enough not to fall for his bullshit. I'll give her that.

Axel orders a shot of whiskey for each of us and she walks off to service the next table. He pulls out his phone and stares at it a good minute before setting it on the table. He's quiet, but I don't miss the way his fingers are twitching against the table.

"What's crawled up your ass tonight, Ax? You've been more of a prick than normal." I eye my brother and watch him squirm.

"Nothing." He shakes his head, but can't look me in the eye. *Lying little shit.*

"Bullshit." Zane voices my thoughts and calls his ass out. "You can't sit still. It's like your dick got hard for the first time or some shit."

"That's not it." He runs a hand over his face and shrugs.

"Well, we ain't got all day. Spit it the fuck out because we're not going ahead with our plans if you can't get your shit together." I need him to be on his game if tonight is to go as planned. The sooner we can hash his shit out, the sooner we can move forward.

"It's Kelsey, alright." He sags against his elbows and goes quiet as the waitress drops off our shots and takes my cue to keep them coming.

"I thought you broke that shit off?" My eyebrows pull together. "You know her dad's the fucking governor. If you're still fucking around, they can use her to find us."

"I did. It's just…" He downs his shot and slams the glass back down against the table. His whole body is wound up tight and I know what's coming before Zane even says it.

I lean closer so he can hear me over the music. "Right now, we're knee deep in shit. Wait until we've finished and then you can bury your dick wherever you want. Got it?"

"That's just it." Axel toys with his empty glass as he glances in my direction. "What are we going to do with *her* when we are done?"

My fists clench as I sit up straighter in my chair. I want to tell him that I'm going to bury her ass six feet under with her father. I open my mouth to do it, but the words won't come out. Flashes of that fucking kiss from yesterday flood my mind. Not to mention a certain morning shower session is still fucking with my head. She may have started out as a vendetta, but now I have no fucking idea. Things are spiraling and changing too fast. It's throwing me for a fucking loop.

"I don't know." I shake my head clear, but Axel isn't done.

"She's been behaving. Maybe you should let her have some freedom or something?"

"You been spending time with her and now you're an expert on what she needs?" My hands clench into fists. I'm not sure why the thought of them spending time together has me ready to break shit.

"No. I just mean sitting in a room all day with nothing to do would be boring as fuck. If anyone would understand that I'd think it would be you, big brother." Axel shifts in his chair, but it doesn't stop him from meeting my gaze head on.

"He has a point, Ash." Zane throws his two cents in.

"I'll think about it." As much as I hate to admit it, they might be right. I need to do something for her. What, I have no fucking clue, but it's something I'll need to worry about later. I have more pressing things that demand my full attention.

"Fair enough."

Our conversation stills as I lean back against my chair and scan the room. It doesn't take me long to find my target. He's got a beer in one hand and a handful of ass in the other as a tall blond leads him through the VIP section. It takes everything I have not to jump over the table and haul ass in that direction.

I down both my shots of whiskey and relish the burn it leaves in its wake as I stand to make my way to the back of the club with my brothers following behind me. I don't have to look to know they're there. They just are. I can feel it.

When we reach the door, we're stopped by one of the bouncers. He's a big fucker, but I'm bigger. Still, knocking him out wouldn't get me what I'm after. So, I pull out a wad of cash between two of my fingers and extend it out to him. He stares at it a minute before he takes it and moves out of the way.

We walk down a dimly lit hall that has nothing but doors on either side.

"How the hell are we going to know which one he's in?" Axel's head whips from one door to the next.

"Pick one." I shrug.

"Are you fucking serious right now?" Axel stares at me like I've lost my mind, and he's not wrong. I've lost more than that and we're here to make up for it.

Axel opens the first door on the left and is met with a girl on her knees sucking off some middle-aged bald fuck. She drops the dick out of her mouth and shouts at him.

"Sorry. Wrong room." He shuts the door like it's on fire and jumps back.

Zane and I lose our shit laughing at his dumb ass. The muscles in my face are stiff at the unexpected movement. It's a simple emotion and yet it feels foreign at the same time. I haven't laughed like that in years, but it feels damn good to be able to do something so normal again. Even if it is at my brother's expense.

"Assholes," Axel mutters under his breath just loud enough for us to hear and that only makes us laugh harder.

We move down to the next door and strike out just the same. It takes a couple more attempts, but we eventually find the one we're looking for. I open the door so fast that the girl riding him doesn't have time to cover herself.

"Get the fuck out of here, man." Luis doesn't even take his eyes off of her pussy long enough to spare me a glance, and what a dumb as fuck move that is on his part.

"Take a walk, sweetheart." I ignore the piece of shit and flash her a wad of cash. She eyes me for a minute then glances at the green in my hand. Money talks. She slides off him, grabs her G-string off the floor and strolls out without a backward glance.

My brothers and I make our way into the room and shut the door behind us. He doesn't even get up from his chair. The dumb fuck.

Zane and Axel make their way behind him while I distract him and keep his attention on me. We need to do this as quickly as possible so we don't attract any witnesses. Messy or not, it makes no difference to me.

"What the fuck you want, Savage?" He pulls out a blunt and lights it up like he doesn't have any fucks to give. The scar under his eye glares at me as an ugly reminder of the loss I felt that night.

"You to put your tiny dick away for starters." My chin juts out toward the limp piece of flesh between his legs.

He grins as he zips his shit up. The cocky bastard is setting me on edge. My fingers itch with anticipation, with the need to wrap around this bastard's throat and squeeze. I suck in a few long, deep breaths to keep my cool.

"We need to talk."

Luis laughs as he takes another hit of his blunt and blows smoke in my direction. "Fuck off, pig."

Zane doesn't waste another second putting him in a chokehold from behind as Axel and I force him to stay seated. His face turns a deep shade of purple as he gasps for air and eventually passes out.

I hold the door, while Axel and Zane put an arm around Luis' limp form and walk him out the back door like he's passed out drunk.

From the time we stuff him into the van until we're dragging his ass out and setting him on the ground, Luis doesn't move. Not even when we strip him of his clothes. He's going to die tonight the same way he came into this world—naked and covered in blood.

Zane turns on the van's headlights so Axel can climb the tree and set up the pulley system he rigged, but covers his eyes. "Ah, fuck. That's in my eyes, Z," he whines like a little bitch.

"You'll live." Zane rolls his eyes and jogs back to where we're standing.

"You know what—"

"Just climb the fucking tree, Ax, or I'll tie your ass up instead."

We pulled deep into the forest a good ways off the road and parked in a spot next to the river that I mapped out earlier, so I'm not worried about any noise. Good thing or I'd be wringing my brothers' necks.

"Fine." He sighs and begins to climb to one of the thicker branches to throw the rope over.

Zane and I drag Luis over by his ankles, not giving one shit if dirt scrapes against him. We tie up his feet and nod for Axel to pull the rope. Luis is suspended by his feet until he's about six feet off the ground and at my eye level. Perfect. Now, it's time to wake his ass up.

"Here. It's river water and cold as fuck. Should wake him up pretty quick." Zane hands me a small metal bucket.

I grab it by the sides and chuck it in Luis' face. He wakes up gasping and shakes his head. It takes a minute for him to get his bearings before he begins struggling to reach up and untie his feet. He never even gets close to reaching the rope. It's a pathetic sight to watch.

"You can try all you want. You ain't getting out of those. Axel can tie one hell of a knot."

"Fuck you, *Puto!*" A vein throbs on the side of his temple as the blood rushes to his face. It's only a matter of time before the ache of pressure hits him.

"The Chattahoochee is pretty cold this time of year. Can you swim, Luis?"

"You're fucking loco, asshole!" His breath comes out in a small cloud of smoke. The mixture of cold water and freezing temperatures is probably getting to him, but I don't give two shits.

"He looks like a damn piñata. Think if we hit him hard enough candy will fall out?" Axel taunts as he drops the rope causing his head to sink closer to the ground. Just when he's about to eat a face full of dirt, Axel stops and yanks him back. He does this a few more times to fuck with him, and I let him have a little fun at Luis' expense.

"Enough, Ax." Zane puts a hand up to stop him from getting carried away.

"You sure? Because I could do this all day." Axel smiles as he pulls Luis back up by his ankles until he's eye level once again.

I ignore Axel, pull my knife out of its holster and stare Luis down. A glint of gold hanging from his neck catches my attention. My fingers pinch the ends of the medallion as my eyes narrow. "Saint Christopher." The tip of my thumb runs over the small engraving a couple of times before I rip the chain off the bastard and clench it in my fist. "You know how we found you?"

He stays silent, so I give him some motivation to speak.

"Your boy, Benny, gave you up." I press the tip of the blade against his throat and he laughs.

"Fuck him." He hocks a loogie and spits near my feet. "He's a pussy. You did us a favor getting rid of his ass." His piss poor attitude grates on my last nerve.

"Hold him," I tell Zane as I take the blade and carve into his chest in hard, slow strokes, each letter a stain on his fucked up soul.

It's as if I'm a painter and his body is my canvas. I can see why Charlee enjoys drawing so much. Creating things by hand takes a special finesse. With every move of my wrist, I slice away into his flesh. Blood drips down his front, toward his neck, as his screams fill my ears, but I don't stop. Not until every letter of Lauren's name is engraved across his chest. He pulled the trigger and took her from me. This is his cross to bear and bear it he will.

"Scream all you want. Ain't nobody gonna hear you this far out." I made sure of that.

When I'm finished carving him up like a turkey, I wipe the blood off my knife with my jeans and step back to admire my handiwork.

His body shivers as beads of sweat drip down the sides of his face. No doubt the cold is making the pain unbearable. Good. Every minute he suffers is one I feel alive.

"You're a religious man, right, Luis?" I toss his Saint Christopher medallion on the ground at my feet. "Welcome to your Garden of Eden." I tilt my head in Zane's direction. He brings the grain sack out of the back of the van and sets it near the base of Luis' head, but hesitates to open it for a second. I almost feel bad for him, but we all have to conquer our demons sooner or later.

"Just find your balls and open it, you pussy!" Axel taunts from his spot in the tree.

"Fuck off, Ax." Zane extends his middle finger in the direction of the tree, but pulls the cloth apart. The second the opening widens we jump back a safe distance. The treats inside slither around, rippling against the fabric. They're angry from being jostled and that's perfect for what I want them to do.

Zane and I are far enough away to avoid getting bitten, but still close enough to enjoy the show. Axel braces against the tree, keeping a firm grip on the rope, and waits for me to give him the go ahead. "Copperheads normally don't attack humans, but let's see if we can prove them wrong."

I flick my eyes to Axel, and he lowers Luis, head first, into the sack. Instead of staying still, the dip shit flays his arms out like a dying fish and draws attention to himself, only succeeding in antagonizing the pit of vipers.

"The more you hit at them the angrier they become, Luis. You might want to remember that."

"Fuck you, *Cabron!*" He ignores my warnings and continues to writhe around the inside of the sack.

Zane lights up a cigarette and stands off to the side watching Luis—who currently resembles a headless worm dangling from a hook—struggle.

"Your saint can't protect you from me. I'll see you in Hell." It's a promise.

Minutes pass as we continue to watch him struggle, watch him fight to live. It isn't much longer before we listen to him take his last breath, just like I listened to Lauren take hers.

Without a word, we cut him down and toss his naked, lifeless body into the river. It bobs from side to side as the current carries it away. I grab his Saint Christopher medallion off the ground and squeeze it in my fist. He won't need it where he's going.

I rub my fingers along the small piece of metal and glare at my brothers. "We have a stop to make on the way home."

CHAPTER
SEVENTEEN

CHARLEE

I'VE BEEN SITTING ON MY bed staring out the large window watching the leaves falling off the trees and trying to think of anything but that damn kiss, and failing miserably. It's stuck on a continuous loop in my head. I'm reliving it over and over. Every single touch is permanently etched into my memory.

His lips shouldn't have been able to manipulate me like they did. I'm angry at myself for giving in to it like I did, for how my body responded to him. It's a betrayal of the worst kind.

The door to my room opens, but I keep my face shielded through a curtain of hair. It's only been a couple of days since I've seen him, which is fine by me. I prefer the distance myself. Every time we're near each other we're like an explosion waiting to happen, a bomb of emotions that'll detonate at the simplest touch.

Dealing with Axel these past couple of days has been much less irritating and stressful. He's the easier going of the three. Whenever he comes in, he greets me smiling or trying to crack a joke. It's a welcome change compared to all of the tension, but I still keep my face blank through it all. If he weren't one of the bastards who kidnapped me and lied to my friend, I would find his southern charm endearing, but he is and here I am. I'm a prisoner in a cage, but I won't be for long. I just need to pick the right moment and I'll be free.

The sound of his feet shuffling on the wooden flooring grates on my nerves. I just want to be left alone to my thoughts. "Go away, Axel. I'm not in the mood for you right now."

"Not Axel." My whole body tenses at that gravelly voice. "Good to know his good ol' boy act doesn't work on you, Princess."

My face hardens when I glance up and meet his stare. His eyes watch me, assessing my mood, and I let him see how pissed off I am.

He steps farther into the room until he's leaning against the wall next to my bed, with his hands hidden behind his back, and watches me. Silence stretches between us for what seems like hours even though it's only seconds. It's a battle of wills to see which one of us will cave first. If he expects me to break it, he has another thing coming. I have a will of steel.

His eyes roam around the room before bouncing back up to mine and I'm not sure I like what I see. It's like he's about to do something that's causing him great discomfort.

Hackles rise on the back of my neck as I brace against the mattress and prepare to defend myself. He's had me all turned around since I woke up here and there's no telling what he'll do next.

He reaches out and I do my best not to flinch, but it can't be helped. I just hope he didn't notice. It's only a slight movement, but judging by the way he's grinding his teeth, I'm thinking he did.

"Here. I brought you these." He sets down a sketchpad and pencil at the foot of the bed and then takes one large step back, giving me some much needed space.

"Why?" I cross my arms over my chest and dip my head to the items on the bed. A part of me is touched at the fact that he knew I would like them, but another is pissed as hell because the only way for him to know such things means he's been watching me for a while.

"I told you, Princess. You're good, you get rewarded." His chin jerks up to the items he's just given me like it somehow makes everything okay and he isn't a manipulative bastard. That has my temper flaring.

I don't fucking think so.

"You think this makes up for everything that you've done to me?" I grab the shit and throw it back at him. It bounces off his chest and lands on the floor next to his feet with a hollow thump. "Well, it doesn't."

"Careful, Charlee." His tongue touches his upper lip as he puts his hand on his waist and glares down at me. A vein on the side of his neck pulses as his temper begins to rise. Join the club, asshole.

"Fuck you! I'm so sick of you treating me like a damn child." He towers over me, but it doesn't intimidate me in the least. I'm too angry to give it a second thought—angry about so many things that I don't know where to start.

He watches me in silence, and I should recognize the calm before the storm, but I'm just done with it all. Done being trapped here like a prisoner. And done being at his mercy.

"Then stop acting like one." His head cocks at me as if I've just proved his point.

"Fuck you! You think I'm some spoiled brat. You have no idea the shit that's happened to me. Being the great Diego Vega's daughter isn't a fucking picnic."

"I know everything there is to know about you, Charlee." He stands taller as his lips curl into a cocky grin, one that doesn't reach his eyes.

"You have no idea how bad things can get, how fast you can have your life stolen from you." A vein on the side of his neck throbs and I know he's close to erupting, but it doesn't stop me from poking the bear.

"Ha! What the hell do you call this?" I jump to my feet and sling my hands out, gesturing to my surroundings. "A fucking vacation?" My feet carry me closer until we're standing toe to toe.

"Last warning, Charlee." His voice comes out low and lethal.

"If you're going to kill me, just do it already. I'm tired of being toyed with." I poke a finger against his rock-hard chest.

He moves so fast that I barely have time to blink. A hand comes up, knocking mine out of the way and gripping onto my wrist as his other hand latches around my throat. His fingers squeeze hard enough to cut off some of my oxygen, but I meet his stare head on. His nostrils flare as his jaw locks.

Emotions flitter across his face, but the only one that stands out front and center is rage. The longer he glares at me, the more unsure I am of whether it's directed at me.

He leans in until we're nose to nose, but doesn't lighten his grip. "You in a hurry to die, Princess?"

The pressure increases until I can feel it build up behind my eyes, but I never look away from his glare. It's another battle of wills. It may get me killed, but I don't surrender. If I die, then I die. I'm at peace with that.

"If it means getting out of here and away from you, then I'll take my chances."

He squeezes even tighter until the room begins to fade into a sea of white noise, and I welcome it. Welcome the numbness that over-takes me and for him to finally kill me, but he never does what I expect.

His lips seize mine in a punishing kiss. Soft, gentle caresses whisper against my mouth, a contrast to the firm grip clutching my throat. All my earlier emotions fade away into the nothingness at the back of my mind. He's eased up enough to allow me to breathe, but that's it. I'm still a prisoner, at his mercy, and yet I don't want to move from this spot. I want more of him. Heat floods my body as his lips work me over and over. He pulls back and I chase—chase more of the high he's giving me. His kisses are a drug, one I can't get enough of.

When his tongue slips inside my mouth, everything inside me explodes. A moan escapes me as I pull him closer. The hardness of his erection digs into my stomach and I'm thankful we're still fully clothed or I'd be making a mistake there would be no coming back from.

I want to feel the heat of his body covering mine.

"Seems like you want to live to me, Charlee." His hard voice is like a bucket of ice on my flaming body.

Shame fills me as warmth blooms across my cheeks. The bastard was playing with me and like an idiot, I fell for it, yet again. "I hate you!"

"Good. I relish in your hate, Princess. You'll do good to remember that." He slams the door shut behind him, leaving me with an unsettling feeling in the pit of my stomach. I may have just screwed up royally and made everything worse.

CHAPTER
EIGHTEEN

Asher

THAT WOMAN GETS MY BLOOD boiling like no one else. I storm out of the room and run right into Axel.

"Whoa. Where's the fire?" Axel skids to a halt, nearly slamming into me.

"That's the last time I take your advice."

"You gave her that?" His eyes dip down to the pencils and paper in my hand.

"Yeah."

"Ash, I know it's been a while, but maybe instead of giving her something that reminds her of your stalking skills, maybe you could get something that's personal for just her."

"Like what?" I light up a cigarette and wait for him to stop laughing at my expense.

"I don't know. Lingerie? They have edible panties and shit." He cocks his eyebrows at me and I want to punch the look off his face. "Taste good, too."

"What the fuck?" My head shakes so hard I'm surprised I don't snap my neck. "No way." I spin on my heels and head toward my room. I'm done listening to him. I don't know why I thought he'd be any fucking help. I have a better idea in mind anyways. My feet carry me to the dresser in the corner of my room and rummage through my top drawer until I find what I'm looking for. I shove it in my back pocket as I'm heading in the direction of the stairs when Axel stops me.

"Going out?"

"Yup."

"If you are, we're running low on food."

"You eat too fucking much." I storm down the stairs with him on my heels. Another thing added to my list of shit I didn't want to do today. I've been so preoccupied combing through the files and gathering more intel from Carl that I haven't left my room the entire day. I'm so close to getting my revenge that I can practically taste Diego's blood on my tongue. It wasn't until a nagging voice inside my head demanded that I go check on the little hell spawn and face her wrath that I even came back to the land of the living.

Zane rounds the corner of the doorway and I drag him along with me whether he likes it or not, because he talks a lot less than Axel.

"Zane and I will be back." I grab my jacket off the coat rack and slip on a pair of aviator sunglasses before adding insult to injury. "We'll need the keys to your truck."

"Why do I have to stay here and play babysitter while y'all go out and get shit? In my truck no less," Axel whines like a little bitch. "If anything, your ass should be the one to stay here."

"Because there's a storm coming and if we lose power you need to be here to handle her." Better him than me right now, but I don't tell him that because I don't want to hear any bullshit about it.

Zane slaps him on the shoulder as he walks off in the direction of the truck without a word. He's been quieter than usual, leaving me to wonder what shit is going through his head, but I don't push because he'll tell me when he's ready. We're the same in that way.

"Why do you have to take my truck when you have a perfectly

fucking good van right there?" Axel waves a hand at the blacked out van parked next to his truck.

"Because that one is stolen and the less we drive it around the better." I pinch the bridge of my nose to keep from wringing my brother by his fucking neck. One day he's going to push me too far. "Just give me your damn keys, Ax."

"Fine." He sighs like a little kid who just got scolded and drops the keys into the palm of my hand. "You better not fuck up Willie Mae or I'll kick your ass." A muscle in Axel's cheek jumps as he points a finger between the two of us. "You hear me?"

"Yeah, yeah. We hear you." I wave my free hand at him as Zane and I climb inside the cab of the truck.

The ride into the city doesn't take us longer than a half hour. Being so far out has its perks, but having to drive a ways just to get more supplies has me second guessing myself on that one. We stop at the first strip mall we see, which just so happens to have a jewelry store right next door.

"Give me a minute."

"I'll meet you inside." Zane nods and walks away without asking me why, but somehow I have a feeling he already knows.

I hesitate on the sidewalk for a minute, second guessing this idea, but something pulls me inside. There's an older woman with graying hair chomping on gum and watching TV from behind the counter as I enter.

"Can I help you with somethin'?" she asks as soon as I approach her.

I pull the small silver band out of my back pocket and set it down on top of the glass case. "I need to get this cleaned."

"This is gorgeous." She eyes the emerald stone that's set inside a small leaf. "Must have been a gift for a very special lady."

"It was." Charlee's mom was very special to Diego, up until her death. I knew it was her mother's and special to her. That's why I took it.

"I'll just take this in the back and it'll be as good as new. You want to wait here or come back later?"

"I'll wait."

"Suit yourself." She smiles at me and walks into the back.

I tap my fingers against the glass and wonder if listening to Axel is even a smart idea. For all I know this could blow up in my face like the last thing I tried to give her.

"That be all for you?" The sales lady brings me out of my head.

"Yes, ma'am."

"All right. Here you are then." She hands me back a gold plastic bag.

"How much?" I reach around to pull out my wallet, but she stops me with a wave of her hand.

"No charge. You just come back and see us the next time you want to buy your special lady another gift." She winks.

"Thanks." I grab the bag and try my best to forget what she insinuated when the headline on the TV catches my attention. A weird sense of unease creeps up my spine as I read the lines. I reach into my back pocket, but my damn phone is back at the house. I was in such a hurry to leave that I forgot it.

Without a backwards glance, I storm out of there and into the grocery store to find Zane. He's not hard to spot. He's the only six-foot tall man with a bun in the whole fucking place.

He has a buggy full of groceries, but the second he sees me his whole body goes on alert. "Everything all right?"

I set the plastic bag on top of the buggy and run a hand through my hair to keep from losing my shit. "Not sure. You have your phone on you?"

"Right here." He pulls it out of the back pocket of his jeans and waves it around in front of me.

"Good, bring up the news feed on your phone."

"Why? What's wrong?" His eyebrows pinch together at my odd request.

"Just do it!" My voice comes out a bit louder than intended, drawing curious stares from other shoppers.

Zane's face hardens at my tone, but he does as I ask. My feet pace back and forth against the dirty linoleum as I try to calm my shit. They weren't supposed to find him yet. We tied him down to keep his dead weight hidden until I wanted him discovered. Timing is everything in order for my plans to work. I know he sees what I did on the TV when every muscle in his body goes ram rod straight.

"Oh fuck."

"Oh fuck is right." I know bodies don't stay hidden forever. I just didn't expect it to pop up this soon, but my gut tightens all the same.

"No way!" A muscle twitches in Zane's cheek and I have a feeling I'm not going to like what he has to say.

"What is it?" My teeth grind together, keeping me grounded to the floor.

"It's not Luis' body that they found." My insides twist into rocks of cement at his words. Something doesn't feel right about this.

"Then who the hell did they find?" My fingers grip the metal of the shopping cart tighter as I wait for him to answer.

Zane shakes his head and drops the one word that has my entire day turning into a heaping pile of shit. "Diego."

CHAPTER
NINETEEN

CHARLEE

RAIN POUNDS AGAINST THE WINDOW as the lights flicker on and off. It's only a matter of time before we lose power. I've survived a Georgia storm a time or two and can predict the inevitable. I lie on my bed staring at the blank wall across from me. The window lost its appeal days ago. Looking out the window at the vast expanse of trees I'll never touch became its own form of torture.

A tray with my untouched food sits on a nearby nightstand as thoughts of Asher fill my head. His ice blue eyes haunt me. Every tattoo has become etched in my memory, like a bad dream—one that turns into something more. Much more. I hate the way my body betrays me every time he's near. It craves his touch, but that's wrong on all levels. He's a monster. One who stole my freedom. I'll be damned if I hand him over another piece of me.

Why does the devil have to look like a God?

Thunder hits so hard that it shakes the whole damn house. The lights flicker one last time before everything goes black. An idea forms in my head and my lips twist into a smile.

I creep out of bed, careful not to make a sound. My fingers dance along the nightstand until the hard plastic hits my fingertips. I dump the food onto my bed and feel my way toward the door. It's not hard to do since there isn't much in here. My body presses against the cold wall as I lie in wait, clutching the tray in front of me like it's my only lifeline.

Footsteps stop outside my door, causing my pulse to race. Adrenaline pumps through my veins, giving me a sudden rush. The second the knob turns, my body hums with anticipation.

"You alright in here, Hellcat?" Not Asher's voice. He steps further into the room and sees the spilled food on my bed. "Shit!" He shines the flashlight around the room. "Where the fuck did you go?"

I slink forward, waiting for the right moment. I only have one shot at this and I have to make it count.

He spins around so fast that he doesn't have time to prepare for my attack. I swing the tray out, slamming it against his face. He goes down with a loud grunt, sending the flashlight to the floor. He's down, but I need to make sure he stays that way for a bit longer, so I lift my foot and kick him right in the balls.

"Fucking bitch!" he groans.

I pick up the flashlight and haul ass through the doorway, out into the hall. His groans echo behind me as I navigate through the hallway. I'm not sure which way to go, but lucky for me it only takes a second to figure it out and find the banister. My fingers slide down the wooden railing as fast as I can without tripping. I stumble a few times, but reach the landing near the front door rather quickly.

More thunder vibrates though the house, sounding much closer this time.

My hands shake as I unlock the dead bolt. Flashes of lightning light up the night sky, causing me to rethink what I'm doing. Then I hear stomps coming down the stairs after me and my decision is made.

"Fuck it," I whisper to myself. It may not be my smartest move, but I'll take my chances. Getting struck by lightning is better than staying locked up in this prison for one more second.

"Get back here. God damn you." His steps pound loud enough to drown out the thumping of my heart.

I bolt out the door without a backwards glance. My bare feet slip against the slick Georgia clay as rain pelts my skin, soaking the over-sized-t-shirt I'm wearing. Cold seeps through, chilling me to the bone, but my arms propel me forward as my legs pick up the pace. The house is becoming a distant memory the further I run. My eyes can make out the faint outline of trees and that's good enough for me. If I make it through there they'll have a hell of a time finding me.

A smile breaks out across my face once I make it through them, but then I realize how fucked I am. Cloud cover makes everything beyond the trees a dark outline. Without the light of the moon, I'm a blind woman running.

My legs begin to feel the exertion as my adrenaline wears off and I slow to a fast walk, but I force myself to keep going. I've come too far to stop now. A whip of lightning streaks across the sky, lighting my way.

I wipe the rain from my eyes and push on. A sudden dip in the ground causes my ankle to twist sideways, sending me forward on my hands and knees. Clay and mud splash into my face. The sharp sting of rocks slicing into my hands is only a slight distraction from the pain radiating from my ankle.

Thunder booms overhead, sending a vibration to rumble straight through me, but it's the high-pitched growl that has the tiny hairs on the back of my neck standing on end. Things are about to go from bad to worse. All I can make out is some sort of animal. It's too small to be a wolf, but sounds too feral to be a dog. Not to mention we're too far out in the middle of nowhere for it to be just a family pet.

My heart beats like a trumpet against my chest the longer I stare at it. Lightening strikes again and I quickly realize just how deep the shit I'm in is. Its mouth is pulled back, exposing a set of sharp canines as a pair of small eyes trains on me. The animal is standing tall and ready to attack any second.

The clay digs underneath my fingernails as I make to crawl back-wards in preparation to run the other way, but I don't even move an inch. Warm hands yank me up to my feet and against a firm chest as another one clamps down over my mouth, muffling my screams.

"Quiet, Princess. I'd hate for either one of us to end up this coyote's dinner." A shiver runs through me at the feel of familiar warm breath against my cheek. It takes a minute for his words to register, but once they do it chills me to the bone.

A fucking coyote? In Georgia?

CHAPTER
TWENTY

ASHER

HER PULSE POUNDS AGAINST THE side of my arm as she takes quick shallow breaths. She's lost inside her head letting the fear take her over. If I don't shake her back to reality we'll both wind up dead.

"I'm going to shove you behind me, but if you run, you die." I probably should have been gentler about my approach, but I can't afford to hold her hand right now. Time is of the essence. This animal is ravenous and the only thing standing between it and its dinner is me. "Understand, Princess?"

She nods against my chest.

"Good girl." I remove my hand from her mouth and with slow, controlled movements, shove her behind me. "Don't move and keep this steady." I shove the flashlight in her hands and aim it in the direction of the coyote.

Fingers dig into the back of my shirt, stretching the wet fabric, as she burrows herself deeper into me, keeping the flashlight where I need it. I ignore how damn good it feels to have her pressed up against me, and focus. In this moment she trusts me with her life and that's not something I'm taking lightly.

My eyes set on the danger in front of us and I puff out my chest. I start yelling for the fucker to leave, showing him that I'm the bigger threat. The coyote merely stares me down, unfazed.

Brazen little fucker.

Looks like I'm going have to resort to other measures. My knees bend down and I grab whatever I can get my hands on. Clumps of mud and nearby sticks fly in its direction. A few hit just in front of the animal, but a few nail him right on the ass. It's one hell of a shot.

"What are you doing? It's going to attack us." Her soft voice melds with the steady pounding of the rain, a perfect staccato to the thrumming of my pulse.

"Relax, Princess. I'm hazing it and showing it that you're mine." I shake off the emotions that one word invokes inside of me and stare straight ahead. There's no time to dissect that now. I'll worry about that shit later. Much later.

After a few more throws, the animal shifts back and forth on its hind legs, finally getting the message. It watches us a beat longer before it finally runs off.

Charlee sags against me, letting out the breath she must have been holding. "Oh, thank God. I thought it was going to rip us apart."

I turn around to face her and my throat goes dry at what I see. The flashlight illuminates every inch of her delicate features. Strands of dark hair stick to the sides of her wet face, highlighting her cheek-bones. Water glistens against her plump lips, making my jeans feel like a noose around my dick.

Her tongue darts out to lick away the stray droplets of water and I have to fight back a groan. Something so innocent is exotic as fuck coming from her. I clear my throat and motion for her to walk back through the trees. Two steps in, she stumbles back.

"You're hurt." My eyes narrow on the way she's favoring her right ankle.

"I tripped over a stupid hole and now I can't put any weight on it." She shrugs like it's no big deal and begins to limp away from me in the direction of the house.

I shake my head at her stubbornness and lift her up over my shoulder into a fireman's carry.

"What the hell are you doing? Put me down!" She slaps at the back of my wet shirt the entire way back to the house.

"Stop being a fucking brat." My hand comes down on her ass with a loud *smack*, shutting her up for a brief second. It doesn't take long for that temper of hers to flare back to life, making me smile. I don't think I'll ever tire of this.

"Don't hit me, you son of a bitch." Her tiny hands clench into fists as she continues to punch at my back while I walk through the house and up the stairs.

"I didn't." I dip my shoulder and adjust her weight so she doesn't hit the back of her head on the doorjamb when we walk through my room straight to the bathroom. "I spanked you. There's a difference."

"You are a such a bastard."

"Stop whining, Princess. I saved you from being eaten by a coyote." I grip the backs of her legs and slide her down my body. The feel of her supple breasts sliding down my chest sends all the blood rushing straight back to my dick. At this rate, my balls are going to be in my throat. I step away giving us some much-needed distance. If I don't get my shit together I'm going to do something we'll both regret. As a distraction, I glance down but that only makes things worse.

"Cold?" My eyes zero in on her nipples. The beady points are poking through her shirt and I envision what they'd taste like against my tongue as I flick on them, sucking each one into my mouth until they're wet and firm peaks.

She folds her arms across her chest to cover herself and I laugh. Her discomfort shouldn't turn me on the way it does, but I'm fucked up enough to enjoy it.

Still holding her tits, she takes the opportunity to do a quick glance at our new surroundings and I wait for her judgment.

Candlelight bounces of the white walls as her green eyes take everything in. I know what's coming the second she opens her mouth.

"It's very…"

Sterile. Clean.

"Austere."

Or that. I shrug it off like it's no big deal, but there's a bigger truth to her words than I'm willing to admit to myself at the moment.

Her body shivers and I know she's going to catch a cold if I don't get her out of these clothes and fast. My fingers grip the edge of her shirt and pull the material up.

"What the hell do you think you're doing? Stop that." She slaps my hands away and cranes her neck back to glare up at me, but not before I see her eyes linger on my chest.

"You're so cold you're shaking. Not to mention we're both covered in mud. So, stop fighting me. The sooner you do, the sooner we can both be warm and you can go back to being the spoiled little brat we both know you are."

I dip my head down to meet her gaze head on. This is a battle of wills she won't win.

"You are such an asshole." The second the words are out of her mouth she flinches. She's expecting me to punish her for this little outburst and I should, but I find her attitude so fucking fascinating this time that I laugh instead.

"I am." If she's expecting an apology, she'll be waiting a long time. Despite her protests, I whip the t-shirt over her head and toss it onto the floor. My body sparks to life with the vision in front of me.

She's standing there in nothing but the white lacy thong and matching bra like an angel for the taking. My eyes linger on her tits. Pert pink nipples are peeking out through the thin strip of lace, taunting me. Every muscle in my body burns with the need to taste, to take what's standing right in front of me.

Judging by the fire in her eyes and the rapid rise of her chest, she's fighting her own emotions. I need to break this connection before I do something we'll both regret. I shove her backwards toward the shower door.

"No." Her whole body trembles as she squeezes her eyes shut. Fear is etched across her face, making me feel like the biggest piece of shit on the planet.

I hold her face in my hands as my thumbs lightly trace circles against her soft cheeks. "Look at me, Princess." When she refuses, I dip my head closer. "We need to warm you up. Can you trust me take care of you?"

"No. I don't trust you at all." Her words hang in the air between us, a somber reminder of just how badly I've fucked things up.

"Fair enough." My lips press into a tight line, hating the truth in her words. Hating that she sees me for the monster I am. I grab the bracelet from my back pocket and place it in her hand. "You will."

Her green eyes narrow at me in curiosity, but I ignore the inkling of emotions that are threatening to break free at what I've done and focus on her wet clothes.

"Let's get you out of these." My fingers dip down to the hook of her bra, but she jerks out of my grasp and steps back.

"I can do it myself."

"Fine." I point to the shower door and work at keeping my face a blank mask. "Clean up and we'll talk."

"You're not going to punish me?" Her eyes narrow as she clutches the bracelet tighter into her tiny palm. She looks as lost as I am at the moment.

"Not this time, Princess." The hardened lines of my face soften. "We have things to talk about, but I'll let you get cleaned up first."

"What about you?" A flush of color spreads across her cheeks and I have to fight back another smile. She too fucking cute like this. "That's not what I meant. I mean..." She hangs her head, unable to finish that thought and I decide to let her off the hook.

"Relax, Charlee." I tilt her chin up until her eyes meet mine. "I'll take one in the downstairs bathroom." With that, I close the door and get the hell out of there before I explode. When I don't hear movement on the other side of the door, I shout, "You've got ten minutes, Princess. Use them wisely."

"Asshole," she mumbles back. My lips twitch at her insult as I change my clothes and head downstairs to the kitchen.

The rules have certainly changed. I just need to figure out if the game is still the same.

CHAPTER TWENTY-ONE

CHARLEE

I HESITATE ONLY A SECOND after Asher leaves before I set the bracelet down on the counter and disrobe. The last thing I want to do is get it dirty since I finally have it back. My ankle hurts when I put pressure on it as I climb inside the shower, but not as badly as when I first fell. The hot water feels like a thousand needles burning against my frozen skin but soon it ebbs away leaving a warm caress in its wake. Mud and debris swirl down the drain along with the last of the aches in my muscles. I contemplate staying in here until the hot water is gone, but I don't want Asher coming in while I'm naked. The candlelight surrounding me only adds to my relaxed mood.

Steam covers the mirror when I step out. I'm able to put a bit more weight on my ankle as I reach for the towel off the rack, which is good, but it's what I find waiting for me on the counter that has me stopping in my tracks. A fresh pair of clothes is resting against the white tile in a neatly folded pile next to my mom's bracelet. It's a bit unnerving to know Asher could sneak in here without me knowing, but I squash those feelings down and dress.

I slip into the red lace thong and discover he didn't give me a bra. Terrific. I knew he'd find some way to punish me for escaping. The bastard. I knew he'd find a way to punish me for trying to escape. When I slip the white t-shirt over my head a faint hint of whiskey and tobacco hit me. This one falls to the top of my knees just like the others he's given me to wear. Never any pants or shoes, though.

A quick glance in the mirror reveals my hardened nipples are very much evident through my shirt. *Terrific.*

For a brief second I debate hiding out in the bathroom all night, but I'm wondering if that was his plan all along. Even still, I don't want Asher to come looking for me. He seems calmer so far and I don't want to push him too far just yet. On the way out, my eye catches the gleam of the bracelet. I shove my wrist through the silver hoop and fight the tears that want to fall. I miss her more than anything. Having it back feels like a piece of me has come back and it settles my nerves some, but I still need to go and face the music for what I've done. With a heavy sigh, I open the door and tip toe down the stairs as best I can with an injured ankle toward the glow of candlelight, where I hear the rumbling of deep voices.

All conversation stalls as their eyes fall on me the second I enter the kitchen. Asher's hair is wet, darkening the brown. He leans against the counter, shirtless, with all of his tattoos on full display. The dim glow from the candles flickers against his golden skin. Smoke from the cigarette resting in between his fingers hovers around him like a halo. It's a sin that the devil looks this mouth-watering.

Feeling exposed, I cross my arms over my chest and that only makes things worse. It only draws his attention right to my chest. There's no missing the gleam of satisfaction behind his eyes. I knew he did it on purpose. I swear I even see the makings of a smile begin to appear on his face, but just as quick as I see it it's gone.

My eyes are drawn to the rippled wall of muscle like a magnet. There's a collage of ink spanning across his chest, but it's the blue lily over his heart with two fallen leaves that catches my eye. Something so delicate and soft is such a huge contrast to the hardness of the man standing in front of me. He's an anomaly, one I'm determined to figure out.

"Have a seat." Zane strokes the ends of his beard with his right hand as he gestures to the open chair between him and Axel. There's nothing friendly about his words, but there's no malice either. He's simply giving me an order.

My eyebrows pinch together as I study him. I'm not sure what I expected when I walked in, but it isn't them offering me a seat at the counter like I'm their guest instead of their captive. Despite the gesture, my feet stay rooted in place. The cold wooden floor is causing the ache in my ankle to throb, but I still wait them out. I'm on edge with this change in dynamics and haven't figured out what their new game is.

"Sit, Princess." Asher's words come out rough and deep. I feel the intensity of it down to my bones. It's enough to knock me out of my stupor.

I nod and hobble toward the black leather chair. The cold of the leather touches the exposed skin of my legs and it's a bit of a shock to the system, but I manage to keep myself together.

"Ankle still bothering you?" Asher's eyes don't miss a thing.

"Hurts a little, but other than that it's fine." My hands clasp together on the black granite counter in front of me as I take in the rest of the kitchen. Everything is black, from the counter to the appliances. The only contrast is that of the dark wooden cabinets. I'm beginning to think Asher isn't fond of colors in general.

The silence is deafening. I feel eyes burning into the side of my face and as much as I try to fight it, I can't help looking in his direction.

Axel adjusts the package of peas resting between his legs and glares at me. A tiny pang of guilt hits me. Perhaps I did more damage than I thought.

"I'm sorry about kicking you in your…" My words die off as I gesture with my right hand toward his junk.

Axel groans, but doesn't say anything else. It seems there's more than one brother who can hold a grudge.

"He's fine." Asher waves off his brother's words.

"Tell that to my aching dick. I think she broke it, man. I'm never gonna be able to use it again." Axel cups the peas closer to his junk. "She kicks like a fucking center back." He narrows his eyes at me and my cheeks burn from the attention.

My teeth dig into my bottom lip as the guilt eats away at me, but given the chance I would do it all over again. I wouldn't be me if I didn't fight for my freedom.

Asher shakes his head at his brother and pours a shot of whiskey. He uses a long tatted finger to slide the shot glass in front of me. "Here, Princess. This'll warm you up and you'll forget all about your ankle."

I toy with the condensation on my glass and stare down at the amber liquid.

"You have done shots before, haven't you, Hellcat?" There's still a bite to Axel's tone, but it's softening up a bit. He may even forgive me for nailing him in the balls by night's end.

My face heats under their scrutiny. "I've done shots before. They're just usually tequila."

"That ain't shit." Axel snorts. "Drink up, Hellcat. It'll put hair on your chest."

Zane watches me and I wish I knew what was going through his head right now because it's a bit unnerving. When I glance over to Asher for reassurance, his eyes are glued to my aforementioned chest.

I cradle the glass in my fingers and decide to hell with it. Things can't get any worse tonight. I toss the shot back in one go. It goes down smoothly, but I'm not prepared for the after effects. Heat burns its way up my throat and lights a fire from the inside out. There's no stopping the cough that escapes me.

"Someone's a lightweight," Axel taunts.

I'm still choking when a glass of water is slid in front of me.

"Drink this and you'll be okay, Charlee." Asher watches me down the water like it's a lifeline.

"Thanks." I wipe my mouth and set the glass back down. The burning has stopped, easing the fire in my stomach. Next time I may opt to eat first.

He nods and rests his elbows against the granite. His blue eyes flicker from his brothers back to me, and that's when I realize something about his posture is off. Gone is the hard ass attitude. If anything he looks frustrated.

"We need to talk, Princess."

All the air is sucked out of the room as I feel all three gazes trained on me. My palms sweat the more they continue to stare in silence. I toy with the bracelet around my wrist to keep my nerves steady. Having a panic attack would be the worst thing I could do right now. He's hesitating. Asher never hesitates. A nervous feeling swirls around in the pit of my stomach

"What is it?" I've never been good at being in the hot seat.

"Just show her, Ash," Axel sighs from next to me.

Zane slides his phone into my line of sight and I'm a bit confused when I read the headline on a news site. Then I keep reading and my world stops with each word.

"No. This is fake. It can't be true." Nausea swirls inside my stomach as my vision spins. Everything around me collapses into a void of nothingness. It has to be a trick. "He can't be dead! He can't be."

The muscles in Asher's cheek twitch as his eyes do something they haven't done before—soften. He grabs my hand and squeezes. "I wish that were the case."

"You're lying!" I cup my hand over my ears, not wanting to hear anymore.

"I'm not."

"You have to be." I jump to my feet ready to make a run for it when the pain in my ankle stops me. The room begins to spin and I'm not sure if it's from the whiskey or all of the pain hitting me at once.

"Charlee…" He moves around the counter to close the distance between us.

"No!" My hands drop into fists at my sides as I glare at him. "Why are you doing this to me? What have I ever done to deserve this?" Numbness takes over my entire body as I sway on my feet and brace a hand against the counter.

Asher doesn't let me be. He grabs me and shoves me against his chest, but I'm so angry I start hitting him. He took those last moments I could have had away from me.

"This is all your fault. I hate you. I fucking hate you!" My fists pound against his chest, while he continues to hold me.

"What the hell?" Axel gets to his feet to intervene, but I hear Asher stop him.

"Let her. She needs this."

I continue to beat him until exhaustion consumes me and I have nothing left. Violent sobs wrack my body as more tears fall down my face. This can't be happening. It has to be a dream. No. A fucking nightmare.

My vision starts to blacken as I lose my balance, but before I can fall I'm swooped up in a familiar pair of warm arms. Asher carries me up the stairs, but I'm too lost in my own head to protest. Maybe time locked in my cage will help ease the ache in my chest? Through my mental fog, I barely notice Asher pass my room and keep going across the hall into his.

I don't put up a fight as he sets me down on his massive bed. I don't move as he pulls back the covers. Not even when he slides in next to me and pulls me into his arms. The warmth of his body does nothing to soothe the cold ache inside of me. I feel dead inside.

He kisses my temple as his fingers lightly stroke my back. "I've got you, Princess."

I cry until I have nothing left. Until I pass out from exhaustion, with Asher soothing me the entire time.

CHAPTER
TWENTY-
TWO

CHARLEE

A COCOON OF WARMTH SURROUNDS me and my body burrows deeper into it. My face is buried into a firm chest. The beat of Asher's heart is a steady crescendo in my ear. The sound should soothe me, but it doesn't. My whole body aches. I feel like I've been put through the ringer emotionally. I watch Asher sleep as a distraction from it all. For the first time since I met him, he looks at peace.

Sunlight beats in through the cracks of the black drapes, giving me an unobstructed view of his features up close. Dark lashes brush against his cheekbones. There's a small dusting of dark facial hair covering the lower half of his face. The crooked ridge of his nose leads a trail down to a perfect Cupid's bow and a pair of skilled lips. Lips that I can still feel pressing against mine.

Remembering what they're capable of has my pulse quickening. A flash of warmth spreads from my chest straight to my core. I clench my thighs together to ease the ache that's building inside of me, but the slight movement is enough to wake him.

Dazed blue eyes meet mine. They're soft and unsure.

"Hi." I don't l know what else to say.

"Hi." His fingers rub against the exposed skin of my hip, where my t-shirt has ridden up, in long smooth light strokes. "You okay?"

"No," I sigh.

"You will be." His eyes wander over my face as he continues to trace his fingers along my skin. "How's your ankle?"

"Better than my heart." Tears pool in my eyes as thoughts of my dad flood my mind. "I hated what he did and wanted to run away from him, from all of it. It shouldn't hurt me like this if I wanted to escape him and never look back, but he was my dad and I was so awful to him the last time we saw each other. If I had known that—" I choke back a sob wanting to break free and force out the rest of my words. "That it would be the last time we spoke I wouldn't have been such a bitch." All control leaves me as I lose it completely. I hate myself for being so weak in front of him right now. I need to be strong and get away from here, not lying in bed with the enemy. But, how can I when the only other person in my life has been taken from me? Kelsey was right. At the end of the day I am a daddy's girl.

The fingers of his other hand reach up to catch a few stray tears that run down the side of my face onto my pillow, but he doesn't move otherwise. He just lies there letting me cry until I'm all cried out once again. It takes me a good minute to pull my crap together.

"I'm sorry." I sniffle.

"It's fine, Princess." He pulls a strand of dark hair out of my eyes and twists it around his fingers.

My heart flutters against my ribs at the gentleness of his actions. They're a sharp contrast to the Asher I'm used to.

We curl deeper into the mattress, staring at each other and letting the silence speak for us, saying so much more than words ever could. His gaze dips down to my lips as the hand on my hip tightens. He leans forward, hovering until our lips are almost touching. He's waiting, asking for permission. I lean my head in, closing the distance between us, granting it without words. My lips tease his with soft gentle kisses, and for a little while he lets me have that one brief moment of control, but it doesn't last long. Bruising and demanding, he dominates me. His tongue collides with mine, a promise of dirty things to come.

Asher breaks away long enough for his hands to trace up the contours of my body, dragging the t-shirt over my head and off to the floor, leaving me in nothing but the red lace thong from last night. He gently pushes me until my back hits the mattress, and nestles himself between my legs.

I let my hips fall to the side, welcoming him in. He's firm all over, which is evident by the hardness of his erection as it presses into my core. The thin lacy material of my thong and his boxers are the only barriers between us. His hips tilt slightly, causing an ache of friction between us.

A small gasp escapes me and I'm rewarded with a smile.

He leans down and sucks a nipple into his mouth. A legion of butterflies summersault in my belly. I drop my head back onto my pillow as my back arches, pushing my chest forward. One hand cups my other breast, pinching the nipple between his fingers and giving it a sight tug. He doesn't stop working me until both of my nipples are pointed into stiff peaks.

The stubble of his facial hair scrapes against my stomach as he drags it downward toward the apex of my thighs. Along the way, his fingers hook into the side of my thong and drag the thin scrap of fabric down my legs. He tosses them onto the floor behind him before his eyes take in their fill of me.

"I need to taste you." Hunger burns bright behind his gaze. His tongue licks up my slit to my clit. He sucks the bundle of nerves into his mouth so hard I have to bite down on my lip to keep from crying out. His tongue continues to lick while the suction of his lips creates a sweet ache inside of me that needs to be filled. He increases the pressure once before letting go with a loud *pop*.

"You taste even sweeter than you smell." The heat of his breath blows against my skin, lighting a match of need inside me.

"More. I need more." My hands come up of their own accord to cup my breasts and begin toying with my nipples.

"More what? Tell me what you want and I'll give it to you." The tip of his nose brushes against my inner thigh as his thumbs bite into the indentation of my hips.

"I want your tongue to fuck me." My breathing is fast and shallow.

"Where do you want my tongue?" He licks up my inner thigh. "You need to be more specific, Princess."

"I want your tongue in my pussy." My hands rest against his broad shoulders.

"Your wish is my command." I feel his smile against my thigh. The wet heat of his tongue thrusting inside of me has my back bowing off the bed.

"Oh, fuck." I writhe against the cotton sheets, moving my hips in tandem with his tongue. Pressure builds slow and deep in my core, spreading through my entire body like wild fire. Not ready for it to be over yet, I attempt to hold back.

"Don't fight it, Charlee. Let go and come for me." His words are my undoing. One last thrust of his tongue is all it takes for my core to clench. My entire body quivers as he continues to tongue-fuck the orgasm from me.

Blood rushes to my face. I sink into the mattress feeling like dead weight. Every limb tingles with pleasure, but he's not done with me yet.

Feather light kisses trail up my inner thigh, up the taut muscles of my stomach, along my breasts, stopping on my lips. He braces an arm on either side of my head, keeping the brunt of his weight from crushing me. His eyelids are heavy and his lips glisten with evidence of my arousal. It's one of the hottest things I've ever seen.

His tongue thrusts inside my mouth, a perfect mixture of him and the musky taste of my juices. My hands brace against his shoulders, running along his spine.

"I need you," he whispers against my lips.

"Take me."

He lines his hips up with my center and presses the tip of his length inside. Inch by inch, he fills me, stretches me, until I feel the bones of his hips digging into mine. "Fuck, you feel good." He groans next to my ear.

"Oh god." My heels dig into the mattress for better leverage. A slight bite of pain registers in my ankle, but I'm so lost in the moment I don't even care.

Asher doesn't just fuck. He dances with his hips, hitting me in places I never knew existed. I've had a couple of partners before him, but none have ever made feel like this. Every thrust hits me harder, deeper than the last.

Beads of sweat drip down our bodies as we become lost in each other. Lost in the moment. A few more deep-seated thrusts have him wringing another orgasm from me. It's even more intense than the first and hits me twice as hard. My body bows and shakes with every swivel of his hips.

Asher continues pounding into me until we're both lost in a fog of sensation. I feel the second he comes. A loud grunt fills my ears as his body tenses underneath my fingers and he twitches inside of me.

I'd like to say that we lie together and come back down from the high together, but that's not what happens. The second he pulls back and looks down at me, everything inside me withers and dies. Something's changed. Disgust is written all over his face.

"Fuck." He's pulling away, both emotionally and physically. He snatches up a pair of gray sweats and walks out of the room without a backwards glance.

I'm left in his bed, naked and alone, wondering what the hell just happened. This was something we both wanted. Or at least I thought we did. Never have I felt so dirty, so used. I dress and stumble back into my room, straight to the shower, noticing for a split second that the power came back on.

Cold water bites into my flesh the minute I undress and step inside, but I let it. I want to wash any traces of him off me.

Asher Savage is a royal asshole. A mistake. One I should have known better than to indulge in.

CHAPTER TWENTY-THREE

Asher

THE SECOND MY HEAD CLEARED and things came back into focus, I knew I was in trouble. I've crossed a line that shouldn't have been crossed. I had to get out of there fast, so I grabbed a pair of sweats and went straight to the basement. It was a dick move, but things would have been much worse if I stayed.

Working up a sweat is the only thing that will put me at ease. I punch the bag until my knuckles are raw and bloody, but never stop. I need the pain. It's what I deserve. Blood pumps in my veins, fueling me on. I'm angry, so fucking angry. Angry at myself for being weak. Angry at her for existing. For being a forbidden fruit I'm aching to sink my teeth into. I can still taste her sweetness on my tongue. She's everything I shouldn't want and yet I crave more. I'm a selfish bastard.

"You all right, big brother?" Zane leans against the wall with his arms crossed over his chest, watching my every move.

"I'm fine," I grunt out as I continue to pummel the fuck out of the bag, each hit coming harder than the last. My limbs are on fire and sweat drips down my chest, but I keep pushing myself.

"Doesn't look like you're fine."

"Fuck off." I'm not in the mood for his bullshit today. My head's a fucked up mess as it is; I don't need his psychology bullshit on top of it.

Quiet stretches between us as he continues to watch. I do my best to ignore him and focus on the target in front of me. Out of the corner of my eye I can see him shifting. My silence is killing him, but that's too fucking bad.

"You can hate yourself all you want. It won't change anything." He can't fucking let it go.

I stop mid-punch and drop my hands to my sides before I spin to face him. He's gone too far. It's time I put him back in his place. "Don't fucking pull that shrink shit on me, Z."

"I'm not." He looks hurt, but I know better. I can see through him.

"Yeah, you are. I was a cop, remember? I can smell that bullshit a mile away."

"We're just worried about you, man. From the time you got out we've done nothing but watch you self-destruct." He toys with the end of his beard, waiting for me to lose it.

"I'm a free man, so quit worrying about me." Blood drips down my knuckles and onto the mat, but I don't feel a thing. I'm numb. Desensitized to it all. Hit after hit, I exhale and take it all out on the bag.

"You're free, but at the same time you're not. You're prison's in here." Zane taps a finger into the side of his head, telling me what I already know. "You can fight the demons out here all you want and we'll have your back the entire time, but until you exorcize the ones in your head, you'll never be free, brother."

My hands freeze mid-punch and drop to my sides as I hang my head. Emotions that I thought I'd buried threaten to surface, but I choke them back down. "It's only been—"

"Six years. We know, but Ash, it's time to start letting shit go. You

can't stay stuck in the past forever. Lauren would want you to live."
He pushes off the wall and walks to stand in front of me.

"I can't! She's dead. They're both dead because of me. Not you.
Me!" I pound a fist against my chest. My throat burns raw from the
strain of it all crashing down on me at once. "How do you think that
makes me feel?" I glare at him.

"You didn't pull that trigger, brother." He grabs the bag, his blue
eyes weary and assessing.

"I couldn't save her, but I can avenge her."

"We'll get all the fuckers who did this." He nods. "I promise you,
but what then? Revenge only feels good for so long until it doesn't."

"It doesn't matter. Nothing else matters." Truth is I haven't
thought that far into the future. I can't.

"That's where you're wrong, Ash. Years from now they'll still be
dead, but what about you? Where will you be? You'll still be alone,
walking around lost and angry at the world. You need to move on,
brother." He grips me by the shoulder and squeezes.

I stare him down, but make no move to acknowledge the bullshit
he's spewing. That would give him the impression he's right and I
can't do that.

"Or maybe you already have and your brain is just too slow to catch
up." He steps back as my head whips up to meet his knowing gaze.

"What's that supposed to mean?" A vein throbs on the side of my
head. My brother's skating on thin fucking ice right now.

"We ain't stupid, Ash. We heard the two of you."

"Leave it alone, Z. This is your one and only warning." The
muscles in the side of my face twitch at the mention of Charlee.
What happened is between us and nobody else.

"No." He shoves me by the shoulder, knocking me back a step.
"I'm sick of watching you self-destruct."

I don't think; I react. My fist comes up and clocks Zane in the
side of the head. His face snaps to the side, but he comes back at me
with a right hook. I shake it off and continue beating his ass. Blood
from my knuckles stains his cheeks with each hit. Adrenaline is
coursing through me so hard that I don't even feel the pain of it.

He swipes my legs out from under me and we end up rolling around the mat, taking cheap shots at each other when we can until he manages to pin me down against the floor.

"Is this what you do now, Ash? You beat the fuck out of anyone who tries to get you to see reason?" He grabs me by the throat and squeezes.

"You know nothing," I grunt out as I struggle for air. Blood rushes to my face, but I don't stop.

"I know Lauren would be disappointed in you." His words burn their way into my skin like a poison.

"Shut the fuck up!" I bring my fist up ready to hit him again when I'm pulled up and onto my feet.

"Enough!" Axel jumps between us and gets knocked down in the process. The three of us end up tumbling around the mat until Axel manages to squeeze in the middle, putting his hands on our heaving chests to separate us. "I said to stop, goddammit. Have y'all lost your fucking minds? The enemy is out there." He jabs a finger to the stairs. "Not in here. Get your fucking heads on straight because shit's getting out of hand. We're family, which means we're in this together."

Blood drips down Zane's mouth, disappearing into his beard. His hair has fallen out of his bun and hangs around his face. Bruises are beginning to form where my fist made contact, and a heaviness settles in my gut. For the first time since I can remember, I feel like the bastard Charlee has known me to be.

"And fuck off for making me sound like the responsible one." Axel continues to ream our asses, and shakes his head like our ol' man used to do.

I fall down against the mat into a sitting position, lock my arms around my knees, and hang my head. Burning from my raw knuckles begins to penetrate and I relish in it. It's my punishment. It's what I deserve. Things have gone from shit to worse today. "I'm sorry. I'm so fucking sorry, brother."

"Don't worry about it." He shrugs and wipes at his mouth. One would think I wasn't the only one looking for a fight.

"Yeah. We knew you needed to either fight or fuck it out and there's no fucking way I'm volunteering for the latter." Axel sits on the other side of me and pretends to cringe.

I don't say anything about the former because I'm not going there. Instead, I slap him in the shoulder hard enough to knock him over.

"You two kiss and make up now?" When Zane and I just stare at him, he takes that as his cue to keep talking. "Good. Moving on. What are we going to do about the Diego situation?" He eyes the both of us. "Someone took him out and carved him up like you did that bitch, Luis. We need to figure out who and fast because something isn't adding up."

He's right and it kicks my ass into gear. There's only one person who can get me the info I need. "Hand me my phone." I dial his number and he picks up on the second ring. Rather than waste time with unnecessary pleasantries, I get right to the point. "We have a complication."

"Yup. I saw the news." He's blunt and to the point. It's one thing I've always liked about him.

"How soon can you get me more info on it?"

He lets out a gasp of air and thinks for a minute. "A couple days maybe. Four max."

"Good. Come to the house on Thursday evening." I end the call and turn to find my brothers watching me.

"You sure he'll come through?" Axel asks.

"If there's anyone I trust more than the two of you, it's Carl. He'll come through."

Zane messes with his hair, throwing it back up on top of his head.

"You need to cut that shit." I jerk my chin in his direction. "In prison, you'd already have a mouth full of dick." My eyes narrow as I cock my head at the glare he shoots me.

"No way." Axel sits up and looks insulted. "I'd be more popular than him." He pulls out a pack of smokes and hands a cigarette to each of us. "They're a little bent, but still work. Like Zane's dick."

Zane flips him off, but still takes the cigarette he's offering.

We light up and sit there for a few minutes enjoying our smokes without speaking. It's the first time the three of us have just sat together like this since my release and it feels damn good. A lump forms in my throat. I've been a shitty brother and need to start doing better by them.

"You know it's okay for you to be happy again." He chews on the side of his cheek as he waits for me to lose it on him all over again.

"Even if she's the enemy?"

"Is she really, though?" Axel asks, giving me a knowing look. One of these days I'm going to knock the cocky out of him.

I open my mouth to snap back to give him shit, but nothing comes out because he's right. I've been so focused on my need for payback that I haven't stopped to see things that were right in front of me.

Shit. I guess it looks like I'll be eating crow twice today and do something I never do. Apologizing.

CHAPTER TWENTY-FOUR

CHARLEE

AFTER MY SHOWER, I SIT on the bed and hug my knees to my chest, letting the hours pass in a blur. My fingers dance along the edges of my bracelet as I watch more dark clouds roll in, an apt reflection of my current mood. My only saving grace is that my ankle feels back to normal. It looks like a bigger storm is preparing to roll in, which is only one of the reasons I didn't attempt to make another run for it. I probably could have gotten farther this time because Asher and his brothers are distracted, but I don't have it in me to move. It seems the news of my father's murder is messing with them as much as it is me. Emotions weigh heavy on me. I've lost my dad and been treated like a whore all within the span of a few hours.

I should run, but where would I even go? I'm all alone; I have no one else. No way in hell would I go back to the house and risk running into Marco, or worse, the she-devil herself, Lola. My body cringes at the thought. That's definitely not an option. I need to stay in here, take the time to figure out what I'm going to do and form a new plan, one that will get me far away from all of this bullshit.

The door opens and I know who it is without looking. If I weren't somehow already attuned to him, the light scent of whiskey would be a dead giveaway. He sighs from his spot against the doorjamb, but I don't take my gaze off the window. I'm still both hurt and pissed as hell at what he pulled with me earlier and don't trust myself not to punch him in the face.

After a few beats, he moves further into the room and sits down next to me. The heat of his body radiates against mine, but I still don't look at him. A pile of clothes is tossed on the bed between us.

"I brought you these."

"Thanks." I keep my body facing away from him. The way I'm feeling he's lucky I don't punch him in the face instead.

"You're pissed at me and I don't blame you. You're going through something, too, and like the bastard I am, I thought of me and my shit first, but I'll make you a deal, Charlee."

Now he wants to make deals? Despite his words, hurt is still shining through front and center. There's no way in hell I'm making it that easy for him. Whatever he wants he's going to have to work for. When I crane my neck ready to tell him exactly where he can shove his deal, the bruises on his face kill all my resolve.

"What happened to you?" The question's out before I can remember I'm mad and not speaking to this jackass.

"It's nothing. Just a slight disagreement with my brothers." When I don't say anything, he continues, "Anyway, like I said before, I want to make you a deal."

"What kind of deal?" My head cranes to the side as I study him for any signs of deception.

"You deserve an explanation about this morning and if you put these on—" he motions to the untouched pile of clothes "—I promise I'll explain everything."

Indecision wars inside of me. I'm torn between being my stubborn self and satisfying my curiosity. In the end, the latter wins out. I grab the clothes he's offered and stomp into the bathroom to change. Going quietly is against my nature and I don't want him to think it'll be that easy to win me over.

A smile spreads over my face when I see that this time, instead of another one of his t-shirts, I'm given a brand new pair of black yoga pants, along with a dark green tank top. I'll take the fact that there's a matching bra and thong set in the same dark green color as another one of his peace offerings. Still no shoes or socks, but it's a start. I should be shocked they're in my sizes, but it's Asher. The man studies every single detail to the letter.

Once I'm dressed and look in the mirror, I feel like a bit of the dark cloud that was hovering around me earlier has been lifted. It's amazing what a new set of clothes can do for one's mood. I leave the t-shirt in a heap on the bathroom floor and walk back out toward the bed.

The mattress dips from my weight, but Asher doesn't move. It's like he's lost in his head. My hands rest in my lap as I toy with my fingers and fight to keep still. I know he'll tell me when he's ready. I just hope I am.

He clears his throat a couple of times, like speaking to me is painful, and it only digs the knife in deeper. Then he does something that surprises me. He talks. "Six years ago, I lost everything."

"What do you mean you lost everything?" The pain I see in his eyes has my heart aching for him.

"Her name was Lauren." His hands clasp together between his legs as he leans against his thighs. "I got home from work one night and found a couple of...*intruders* inside. They shot and killed her. She was...she was eight months pregnant."

I put my hand over my mouth to fight back the bile of vomit creeping its way up my throat. Then my eyes glance down to his green t-shirt as if I can see what's hidden underneath. "The lily tattoo on your shoulder." I knew it meant something to him.

"Her favorite flower."

"And the fallen leaves?" I ask, already knowing the answer.

"For Lauren and our baby—the two lives that were stolen from me that night."

"Oh, Asher." Just when my heart couldn't break anymore for him, he tells me more.

"They found me covered in her blood and thought I did it. I was convicted of the voluntary manslaughter of Lauren and our unborn child. They gave me seven years. Seven years for killing my wife and son." He shakes his head in disgust. Before I realize what I'm doing my hand is on his thigh, squeezing for support, and encouraging him without words to tell me more. He's so lost in the memories that he doesn't even notice my touch. "Because I was a cop and had no other records, I was out in six."

"I'm so sorry, Asher, for all of it." An inkling in the back of my mind has me putting the pieces together, but I need to hear him say it. "Did you ever find the men responsible?"

The muscles in his throat contract as he takes in my watery eyes, but what he doesn't do is answer my question. Instead, his eyes glance down to the hand that's squeezing his thigh as if my touch burns him, and his eyes narrow. Feeling foolish, I move to pull my hand back but he stops me. His fingers lace through mine as he stares down at our joined hands. He sighs and leans in until his forehead is pressing against mine. We sit connected like this, enjoying the silence. Neither one of us makes a move to take it any further. In that moment it's just he and I. All the other bullshit fades away until the sound of his brother's voice shouting from downstairs breaks it.

"Yo, I'm starving! Y'all coming down here or what?"

"Give us a minute, Ax!" Asher shouts back and then asks me, "You hungry, Princess?"

Right on cue, my stomach growls loud enough for him to hear. I want to die of embarrassment.

"I'll take that as a yes." Asher's hand squeezes mine one more time before he's pulling me to my feet and leading me out the door to an unexpected fate.

CHAPTER
TWENTY-
FIVE

ASHER

C HARLEE NEVER LETS GO OF my hand as I lead her down stairs, and I do my best to keep my eyes off of her tits. That outfit may have been a mistake and I'm going to kick Axel's ass for telling me to buy it. The soft material hugs all of her curves, drawing attention to her phenomenal body; a body my tongue had licked and fucked every inch of. Traces of her sweetness still linger in my mouth and I have to think about something else before I walk into the room, my dick trying to jump out of my pants.

All conversation dies as we enter the dining room and rain continues to ping against the roof. My brothers take us in, stopping on our joined hands. Zane meets my gaze and winks, but doesn't say anything, which is good because he'd get another ass beating if he did.

Charlee hangs back a step, shuffling from side to side. She's no doubt nervous and assessing Axel's mood today, which is unnecessary. He has one of the shortest fucking attention spans I've ever seen and was over what happened the second she found out about Diego last night.

Her hand squeezes mine and I hear the slight intake of breath as she gets a look at the bruises on Zane's face that I'm sure match my own. My fingers curl deeper into hers, reassuring her without words that he's fine and that's not me being a cold-hearted prick. He really is.

As brothers, we fight and we forgive. It's what we do.

Speaking of the bastards, both of them are cocking their eyebrows, watching us and our joined hands. Bits of our earlier conversation roll around in the back of my mind, but I do my best to forget about it. It doesn't stop me from hearing them gloat from here.

Axel kicks out a chair with his foot and lifts his chin to Charlee. "Y'all gonna sit down or stand there and stare all day?"

Charlee spares him a glance but her feet stay firmly planted on the floor, so I make the decision for her. I tug on her hand, pulling her forward, and plop her tight ass in the chair. I loosen my grip to take the empty one next to her and immediately feel the loss of her warmth.

"You doing okay, Charlee?" Zane asks. I sit up tighter in my chair as he does. It's the first time he's really initiated any type of contact with her and I'm wondering if the talk in our basement was as much about me as it was about him.

Charlee ducks her head down to the table as she nods, a gesture that doesn't sit well with me. She's always been so full of fire that I hate seeing her this way. My thumb lifts her chin until she has no choice but to meet my gaze.

"How do you really feel, Princess?"

"He was my dad." She shrugs as tears pool in her eyes. Her words hang in the air between us like dead weight.

I drop my hand over her chair and rub small circles against her back. There's nothing we can add. I hated the bastard for what he did. If he hadn't ended up dead I was planning on ending him myself, but she knew an entirely different version of him that she's mourning the loss of.

"Did the article say if my stepmother was found with him?" Her voice cracks at the end of her question.

"No, but I have a friend looking into it for me. I'll let you know what he finds out."

She nods and hangs her head once again. The three of us just sit there and stare at each other like a couple of idiots. We're at a loss for what to do. If it were one of us we'd beat it out of them, but this requires a different approach altogether.

Axel breaks the silence, snapping his fingers like he's just come up with the best fucking idea ever. "You know what you need? A nice traditional southern dinner."

"You can cook?" Charlee's head tilts up as she asks and the look on my brother's face is priceless.

"My mama taught me. A boy's gotta eat things other than pussy once in a while, Hellcat." He winks as Zane smacks him over the head.

"What the hell, man?" He rubs at the sore spot and shoots Zane a death glare.

"You're a fucking idiot." Zane shakes his head. "Ignore him, Charlee. We dropped him on his head as a kid."

Axel flips him off. "Just for that, I ain't feeding your ass shit tonight."

Zane just rolls his eyes. He isn't even fazed. Neither am I. Axel's made the same threat for years and we know enough to know he's bluffing.

"What's a traditional southern dinner?" Her dark eyebrows pinch together.

"How the hell do you live in Georgia but you ain't ever had one before?" Axel damn near falls out of his chair at this news.

"I wasn't born here. We moved here after my mother died when I was a teenager." Charlee chews on her bottom lip, causing my dick to take notice. I adjust myself as nonchalantly as I can and do my best to focus on this little bit of information she's sharing. It was in the file I have on her, but it's different hearing it from Charlee herself.

"That's an outright crime." Axel shakes his head like it's the end of the world and strolls into the kitchen.

Charlee shrugs and continues to fidget with her fingers. Axel's trying to put her at ease, but she's still on edge and unsure around us. Not that I blame her. We've done much to convince her otherwise.

"No one should ever go without tasting the deliciousness of soup beans, greens, and cornbread with onions and ketchup." Axel rubs his hands together like he's just solved world hunger. "Why don't you grab the greens out of the fridge and help me, Hellcat?" he asks, as he begins to dice an onion. He's playing it smart for once, distracting her and not pushing for more details.

"Um, sure." Charlee makes her way to the fridge and my eyes stayed glued to her backside the entire way there. When her ass bends over in those tight as fuck yoga pants, everything inside me stirs.

Why did I buy her the damn things?

The sound of Zane clearing his throat has my eyes shooting up to meet his.

"What?"

"Nothing." He shakes his head and gives me a knowing look that I want to smack off his face as he takes out a cigarette and lights up.

I do the same, and we sit at the table for a few minutes enjoying the show of Charlee and Axel cooking. It's obvious Axel's enjoying playing teacher, but he's getting too handsy for my liking. If his hand 'accidentally' brushes up against another part of her I'm going to chop it off. Brother or not, he'll make do with one.

"You think whoever took out her old man could be after her, too?" Zane asks as he pinches his cigarette between his fingers.

"It's a possibility." One I've been rolling around in my head over and over since we first read that damn article. Something about it isn't sitting right with me, but I just can't figure out what.

"What are we going to do about it?"

"I don't know." I scratch the side of my face and shift in my seat. Having this wrench thrown in my plans has me at a standstill. "We'll wait and see what Carl finds out. Then we'll go from there."

"Ash, you can't keep her locked up your prisoner forever. And judging by the way you keep eye fucking her I'm thinking our talk was somewhat effective?" He exhales a cloud of smoke and flicks his head in Charlee's direction.

I blow mine in his face without answering him. It's nobody's business but my own what I do with her. He may have given me the push, but I'll take the steps on my own, in my own fucking time.

"That's it, Hellcat. Now we need to let it sit for a couple of hours." Axel's voice brings our attention back to them. The little shit is giving me a smug grin as he wraps an arm around her neck in a hug.

My fists clench as I struggle to keep from hopping the counter and beating his ass. He always has to push my buttons. The fucker. He's lucky Charlee's standing next to him because I wouldn't hesitate to do it otherwise, but I won't risk having her hurt in the crossfire.

Then another thought comes to me. Whoever did this could be coming for her next, which means she's even more vulnerable without Diego's protection. Without a word, I put out my cigarette, shove my chair back, and walk over toward them.

Axel wears a shit-eating grin the whole time he watches me and whispers something in her ear that has her throwing her head back in a laugh. That's it. He's gone too far. I grab the thumb of the hand braced against the counter and pull it back.

"Ow, fuck!" He yelps like a little bitch and drops his arm. I may have pulled harder than necessary, but it's not like I broke it or anything. He'll live. He'll also remember to keep his damn hands off her.

"You okay?" Charlee looks up from what she's doing at the sink.

"He's fine." I answer for him and take her by the hand. "Come with me."

"Where are we going?" Charlee's wary eyes meet mine as she stumbles to follow me.

"Basement." Guilt seeps into my gut the second I feel her hand stiffen in mine. "Relax. You're safe, Princess. I promise." Granted, the last time I took her down there it wasn't under ideal circumstances. Things are different now. I'm hoping she'll trust me a little bit. I need to convince her that I'm the monster she's safer with at the moment. Convince her that things will be different starting now. For both of us.

CHAPTER
TWENTY-
SIX

CHARLEE

MY HEART POUNDS IN MY chest as we enter the basement. The last time I was down here I was tied to a chair, and I'm not keen for a repeat of that. Asher wants me to trust him, but he hasn't given me anything to prove I can.

He leads me onto the mat and drops my hand. "Can you fight, Princess?"

"A little."

"Take that off and show me." He dips his head down to the bracelet dangling around my wrist.

"Right now?" My eyebrows pinch together as I do what he asked. I'm not sure what I expected when he brought me down here but it wasn't this. He continues to stare at me and I shift on my feet. I hate being put on the spot like this. "You can't be serious?"

"Never been more serious about anything in my life. Shit's going down, Charlee, and I need to know you can do something to defend yourself, to get away if needed."

"What kind of shit?" That has my full attention. A nagging suspicion creeps its way into my throat. Something about my current circumstances has changed and I don't just mean between Asher and myself. Ever since he showed me the article about my dad's murder, he's been sticking to me like glue and now he wants to teach me to protect myself. It doesn't add up.

"Nothing for you to worry about just yet." He shrugs his shoulder and continues on without letting me pry for more information. "We know you're good with clawing the shit out of people and…" He stops talking long enough to do something I haven't ever seen him do —smile. "Axel knows all too well how good you are with those legs." His eyes dip down to my yoga pants as his smile drops. His throat bobs up and down so hard I can feel the violent motion from here as if he's swallowing me whole. The way his gaze is fixated on my legs is doing things to my insides. I clear my throat to bring his focus back to the here and now. It takes a couple of tries before he's finally able to pull his gaze from my legs.

"Show me what you've got." He puts his hands up and does a typical boxer stance.

"Fine." I make a fist and slam it into the block of muscle that is his chest. Pain radiates up my hand the second I make contact. "Ouch." I shake out my hand to will away the discomfort.

"You call that a hit. That wasn't even a fucking tap."

"Speak for yourself, asshole." I flex my hand a few times to tamp down the pain as my temper flares. He's pushing my buttons and I want to smash in his big stupid face right now. "It's not a fair fight. You're like a foot taller and a block wall of muscle." I know I'm whining, but I don't give a damn right now. My annoyance at him is stronger than any common sense.

"You think the asshole who attacks will give a shit if it's a fair fight?"

"No."

"Fuck no. Most guys are stronger than you, but you have to be smarter. You've got the fire, but you freak out and let your panic take over every time. That's the worst thing you can do. Focus on your breathing or whatever you have to do to keep your shit together, and take the fucker down."

"No way. This is stupid." My head twists to the side so he can't see the eye roll I'm giving him.

"Don't roll your eyes, Charlee, or I'm going to spank your tight little ass red."

Well, shit.

"I need to know if you can fight back and do what you can to get away somewhere safe." I hate when he's right and makes sense. "Try again."

I do as he says, but much to the same sad results. Again and again, we keep going until my arms feel like they're going to fall off. I wipe the sweat off my brow and let out a deep exhale. "I can't do anymore."

Asher isn't done with me yet, though, not by a long shot. His stamina isn't normal. My mind slowly drifts to what other areas that kind of agility transpires to, but all thoughts are halted by him grabbing me by my shirt, throwing me onto the mat, and climbing on top of me. He pins my arms.

It takes me a minute to gather my wits, but when I do I'm seeing red. "What the hell are you doing? Let me up right now."

He ignores me and forces his body between my legs. "Most of the time they'll throw you to the ground and do this."

A shocked gasp of air leaves me as I adjust to the heavy weight bearing down on top of me.

"Try to get away from me." His words come out deep and rough, grazing across my skin, and there's no missing the undercurrent of warning they hold. He may be telling me to try, but it's clear that I'll never get away from him. When I make no move to attempt such a thing, he snaps out, "Charlee."

"Fine." I twist and squirm, but he's not budging. My feet plant against the floor for better traction as my hips rock from side to side in hopes of shifting his weight. That turns out to be a huge mistake for both of us. Every movement causes the thin fabric of my yoga pants to rub against my clit and I feel him hardening right against my core. Each swivel of my hips has those sensitive nerve endings sparking to life. I have to bite my lip to keep in the groan that wants to break free, and force myself to concentrate on throwing him off me instead.

A couple more tries end with the same results—him still on top of me and a throbbing core that's about to explode. Asher's nostrils flare as he takes a few slow deep breaths. He's struggling as much as I am, but for an entirely different reason. Sweat drips down both our faces as we fight the exhaustion that wants to break through from the close contact, but I don't quit trying. My hips buck up one last time with everything I have and he still doesn't move.

"I can't."

"You're too focused on creating distance. Don't be afraid of bringing me in closer. Bring your legs up—" his hands grip the backs of my thighs and slide them up his body "—and squeeze."

My body goes rigid for a second before relaxing into his hold. Flashes of where those strong hands have been has fire sparking deep inside my belly and spreading like wild fire across the rest of me. I've never felt so naked. So exposed.

"Squeeze me, Princess," he growls.

I clench my thighs slightly around his waist and try not to think about anything else fighting the urge to clench as well. The move brings my ass flush with his hard cock, causing a flush of heat to flood my body. Lucky for me I'm already running hot from what we're doing so he won't notice.

"That's good, but this time I want you to grab my wrist and arch your body back with my arm, as you do it."

I follow his instructions, but don't put my full weight behind the move for fear of pulling his shoulder out of its socket. "Like this?"

"Good. If it's anyone but me, you do that with everything you have. It'll dislocate their shoulder and give you a better chance to get away."

"Well, that was fun." My body relaxes against the mat, ready for this to be done and over with. The stretchy cotton fabric of my pants is starting to stick to me and I desperately need a shower.

His body squirms between my legs, sending a shockwave of sensation through me, but he doesn't make to get off me. "You want to go, go."

My arms push against him but he doesn't budge. "I can't with you on top of me like this."

Hands wrap around mine, holding them there as his blue eyes darken. My breasts crush against his chest with every panting breath I take. All oxygen is sucked out of the room, as it becomes a raging inferno of hormones, sweat, and sex.

"Get me off, Princess," his exerted voice whispers against the shell of my ear. Those words hold a double meaning. The hardness of him presses against my core and it has me hot and sweaty for completely different reasons.

The weight of his body comes down on me, pinning me in place. I plant my feet on the ground and push off with everything I have until we're turning and he's flat on his back with me straddling him.

"Holy shit. I did it!" My hands fist in the air as I take a moment to enjoy the fact that I've just gained the upper hand. It doesn't escape my attention that he let me win this time, but I don't care. A win's a win. When I glance down, I expect Asher to look happy with this, but I see something else entirely flash across his face.

"What are you going to do with me now, Princess?" His fingers rest on the tops of my thighs, right next to the indentation of my hips as he watches them stroke small circles.

"Since I'm on top, does that mean I get to decide?" We're not even talking about fighting anymore.

His hands tense at my words, but I don't wait for him to answer. I'm not sure what comes over me. It could be that I'm lost in the moment or that I feel like we've just had the most intense game of foreplay, but I slide down his body until my face is flush with his groin.

"This." I pull down his jeans, springing his hardened cock free. Asher is by no means a small man and his dick is no exception. It's a bit intimidating. His swollen mushroom tip is red and already dripping with pre-cum. My mouth waters at the sight and I don't wait another second to take him in my mouth until he's hitting the back of my throat.

"Fuck, Princess," he hisses out between his teeth.

I moan as the salty taste of him coats my tongue. I pull back until he's almost all the way out and suck him back in. My head bobs up and down in a slow, torturous rhythm, relishing in every groan I suck out of him.

His hands grip the sides of my hair as he begins to thrust his hips faster and faster. I keep the rapid pace he's setting and flick my tongue along the underside of his cock.

A gag has my eyes watering, but I don't stop. I continue to suck him deeper and deeper. Saliva drips down the sides of my mouth, onto my chin, and I revel in the feel of it. My eyes glance up, and the look on Asher's face is one of the hottest things I've ever seen—head thrown back, mouth lax, eyes closed. Having him at my mercy for once has warmth pooling in my panties. I become lost in enjoying the taste of him.

"Stop, Charlee." He pulls my head away and flips me onto my back. In the blink of an eye our clothes are gone and he's slamming into me in one quick thrust.

I'm so wet and ready my toes curl the second he grinds his body against my clit. "Yes."

"You like my dick, Princess?" He pulls back only to thrust back in so hard my eyes roll back in my head.

"I do. I really do." My back arches, coaxing him even deeper inside me.

His hand comes between us and his fingers go right to my clit. A cacophony of fireworks explode inside of me the second those soft fingers play me. "This pussy is mine. Let me hear it."

"It's yours." My heels dig further into the mat as my pelvis grinds up to meet him thrust for thrust.

"You're fucking right it is." His teeth sink into my chin, biting me, marking me from the inside out. He slams into me a couple of more times and the orgasm that hits is so hard I can't breathe.

I hold my breath and ride it out as he continues to slam into me.

He bottoms out one last time and I feel him twitch inside me with his own release.

He collapses on top of me and we lie there letting our breathing even out. No words are spoken, but they're not needed. The first time was an impulse. This time there's no denying what we've done. I just hope it's not a means to an end and I'm not the one left broken.

CHAPTER
TWENTY-
SEVEN

CHARLEE

ONCE WE'RE DRESSED, WE WORK out for a few more hours until Zane calls out to us that dinner is ready. That's like music to my stomach. I've worked up an appetite. On the way up the stairs, a thought occurs to me.

"You don't think they heard us, do you?"

Asher presses a quick kiss to my forehead and tugs on my hand. What he doesn't do is answer my question.

When we walk upstairs, Axel has the table all set and food served. He hasn't said anything yet, so I'm holding out hope there's a chance they didn't hear us in the basement. He gestures for me to take the seat at the table across from him, and Asher sits to my right. Everything smells so good that I don't waste time digging right in. I don't remember a time when I was ever this famished. It isn't until I'm through my second mouthful that I realize I'm being stared at and no one else is eating.

"Hungry, Princess?" Asher asks.

"You worked me pretty hard." I shrug and take a mouthful of the greens on my plate.

"I bet he did." Axel flashes me a blinding smile and I choke on the bitter taste filling my mouth. It's official; I am not a fan of collard greens. Nopales all the way for this girl from now on. "You all right there?" His eyebrows pinch together.

I manage to grunt out a scratchy, "Fine," and wash down the rest of the collards with my glass of water. Axel balked at the fact that I wanted just water, but after the workout Asher put me through I needed the hydration.

Heat floods my face as I feel Axel's stare burning into me. I knew they heard us. Most people wouldn't even bring it up. Not Axel. Nope. I've discovered he's the one who likes to find out what your buttons are and push them constantly. Rather than be embarrassed, I decide to take the opportunity to find out more about them.

"Were you a cook in the military?"

"How did you know I was in the military, Hellcat?" Axel cocks his head to the side at my question. "My big brother spilling all our family secrets?"

"It was a guess." I shrug. "Kelsey's older brother has a similar tattoo to the one on your arm." The second I mention my friend's name, the food in my stomach turns. I've been so distracted with what's happening that I haven't had a chance to ask about her. There's no missing the way Axel's demeanor changes at the mention of her name either. "Have you talked to her?"

"No." His eyes shoot to Asher before coming back to me as his hand clenches into a fist. "I haven't."

"We were both Navy Seals. We joined together after our parents died." The mood in the room changes the moment Zane mentions their parents. Somberness floats through the air around us like a black cloud and he must see the questions burning behind my eyes because he answers them. "They were killed by a drunk driver coming home from their anniversary dinner."

"Oh, I'm sorry." A pang of sympathy settles deep in my gut. "I didn't mean to…"

"It's fine, Hellcat." Axel tries to reassure me, but his smile is forced.

"My mother drowned in our family pool when I was thirteen." I feel the need to let him know that I really do understand their situation. That's the only explanation I can think of as to why I reveal what I do. "My father ended up marrying one of the girls he met at college my freshman year."

"Ouch. That's brutal, Hellcat." Axel's face is relaxed, but there's no missing the sympathy in his gaze.

"That must have been hard to deal with being so young." Asher watches me closely like the mention of my dad's death is going to have me falling apart. Little does he know I'm much stronger than that. One meltdown is all I'll allow myself before I push through. Anything less and my father would be disappointed.

"It was. She was a very good swimmer, so it's always made no sense. When I asked my dad, he said she was drinking and hit her head on the side before she fell in."

Quiet surrounds us as we pick at our plates. I have a feeling I've hit a sore subject and made dinner awkward for everyone.

Zane takes pity on me and breaks it. "The cameras are done for. When the storm knocked out the power, it fried the whole system."

Asher tells him he'll take a look later and the rest of dinner isn't as deep of a discussion as it began, and for that I'm grateful. Instead of being the one in the hot seat, I listen and watch them interact with each other. The conclusions I come to are fascinating.

The three of them couldn't be more different. Asher is the oldest and the protector in the family. Axel is the typical goofball baby brother, while Zane is still a bit of a mystery to me. He appears to be more of an observer and the voice of reason, but he's also harboring secrets of his own—secrets that reflect the bit of darkness behind his eyes.

After dinner, we head upstairs and call it a night. I make to go back to my room, but Asher pulls me into his. We shower and fall onto his bed. Both of us are exhausted from the day and fall asleep in minutes.

Over the next couple of days, things shift between us. Gone is the fear and hate I've felt for him. I'm not sure when or how it even happened, but I no longer have the desire to run away. Between Asher comforting me over the loss of my father, to him sharing his own demons with me, we've grown much closer.

Our days have been spent walking around the property, and if he's too busy doing other stuff I'm not yet privy to, I spend my time with Axel in the kitchen showing him some of my favorite childhood dishes. It's a stark contrast to how things started and I'm enjoying the change. I've been so busy that I haven't had time to dwell on the death of my father. If I didn't know better, I'd say that this was their plan all along.

The nights have been spent together in Asher's bed, having tons of salacious sex and sleeping in until Axel decides we've been there long enough and threatens to join us unless we come downstairs into the land of the living. I'm asleep in Asher's bed when a pained grunt wakes me. He's thrashing against the blankets and saying "no" over and over again. Watching him struggle is like a stab to the heart. Sweat dampens his forehead as he continues to fight his demons.

"Asher. Wake up!" I shake him as hard as I can, but it turns out to be a mistake. His hands shoot up and wrap around my throat, squeezing. I choke and gasp for air as my hips thrust forward in a sad attempt to buck him off of me, but it's no use. I'm helpless.

Pressure builds behind my eyes the longer I'm deprived of oxygen. My hands slap at his to wake him, but he's stuck so deep inside his nightmare there's no pulling him out of it. Blackness swallows my vision, threatening to pull me under. Desperation kicks in and I scrape my fingernails along the tops of his hands, drawing blood.

Asher's eyes snap open and the moment he registers what's happening, his hands drop away. Ragged breaths leave him as his gaze locks with mine.

"Fuck!" He punches the headboard hard enough to crack the wood in half. His knuckles split open and blood drips down onto the mattress next to my head.

I push him away and stumble out of the bed, needing to put some space between us. My heart pounds against my chest as I reach for my throat with shaky fingers and rub away the slight burning sensation that lingers.

"I hurt you." It's a question, not a statement. He sits up on the edge of the bed and runs a hand over his head. His blue eyes darken the second they land on my neck. It's as if he's still seeing his hands wrapped around it and I swallow down the lump I feel forming in my throat.

"No, but just…" I hold up a hand and try to gather my thoughts as to what the hell happened, but when I look over at him what I see has my stomach plummeting.

There's a far off light in his eyes and he looks so lost. I feel if I don't try to snap him out of it, he's going to shut down and take off on me again.

My hands come to his face as I close the few feet separating us and stroke the sides of his cheeks, begging him to come back to me. "I'm scared, Asher, okay. Let me have a minute to process all of this. I'm not leaving, but I can't lie with you if I have to worry about you attacking me in your sleep."

His eyes meet mine and the pain behind them has my heart splitting in two. "I could have killed you."

"But you didn't."

"Not this time."

"It was just a bad dream." I refuse to believe he'd hurt me intentionally. Maybe the Asher I first met would have, but not the one I've come to know these past few days.

"No, it wasn't." He shakes his head. "And that's the fucking problem." I want to ask him about it, but the wall that slams down over his eyes has my lips staying firmly pressed together.

"All right, break it up, you kids." Axel pops his head inside, breaking our connection, but Asher never moves his gaze away from mine.

"Fuck off, Ax. Or I'm going to kick your ass."

"Just thought you'd want to know you have a friend over. Should I tell him you're *busy*? I mean, it is almost noon, but I'm sure he can wait." Axel continues to taunt Asher and I have to fight back a laugh. Somehow I get the feeling that as the youngest, he does this a lot.

"I'll be right down."

"You sure? I can always wait here in case you need any help." Axel's footsteps only make it past the threshold before Asher's voice stops him.

"Ax." He doesn't find his brother anywhere near as amusing as I do.

"I'm going." Axel puts his hands up and heads back the way he came.

Asher pushes off of me to a standing position and holds his hand out to me. "Come with me?" For the first time since I've been here, he gives me a question and not an order. That's the only reason I curl my fingers around his and allow him to lead the way. Or at least that's what I tell myself.

CHAPTER TWENTY-EIGHT

ASHER

THE SECOND WE ENTER THE dining room and see them sitting at the wooden table, Charlee's steps stop. She studies the newcomer in the room, Carl, with rapt attention, and I know what she sees.

His dreads hang down to his shoulders touching the top of his white t-shirt. The snake tattoo that's embedded in his dark skin is the next thing that usually catches attention, and judging by the way her eyes are going right to it, I'm right with that assumption. It's something I've picked up on that she tends to do in new environments. Diego taught her well. She pulls on my hand to let her go and fade into the background, but that's not going to happen.

Her weight shifts from one foot to the other as she hesitates, so I make the decision for her again. I sit and pull her down into my lap, bringing my hand down to rest against her thigh. Her body stiffens at the movement but quickly relaxes when my thumb starts rubbing small circles against her. She squirms and I realize what a mistake this was. Having the heat of her body so close to my dick has it once again taking notice and standing up in appreciation. I force all thoughts of her perfect ass and what I'd like to do to it out of my head and focus my attention on Carl.

"Glad you made it." I keep my conversation light and ominous because I'm not sure if I want Charlee to hear what he's found out. It's best to vet the information myself and decide from there.

"Sure thing." He nods, not paying me the least bit of attention. His gaze is solely focused on Charlee, trailing down her body to that tight as fuck white tank top that's doing nothing to hide the black lace bra underneath. This lasts a second too long for my liking and I'm suddenly wishing I'd just given her another of my shirts to wear. I lift my hand higher and wrap it around her neck, pulling her back up against my chest. This earns me a laugh from both him and Axel. If Zane has an opinion on this pissing contest, he's keeping it to himself.

At least Charlee doesn't stiffen under my touch anymore, and it's a good thing because I can't keep my fucking hands off of her right now. It's like she's the beacon keeping me grounded. I don't want to think what that means just yet and squash this feeling from going any further.

"How's hunting season?" Carl props his elbows on the table and leans against them, but doesn't drop the shit-eating grin he's sporting. Even though I'm irritated, I don't miss that he's testing me to see how much Charlee knows and what he can mention in front of her.

"It's good. Only need one, maybe two more and I'm all set." I look him dead in the eyes and he catches on to what I'm saying.

"Well, it is fall. Most of the big game is indoors." I pick up on his clue immediately. The next piece of shit on my list is hitting the Viper's Den tonight. After that tidbit, we shoot the shit about nothing at all until I manage to get Axel's attention from over the top of Charlee's head. His head cocks to the side, pretending he doesn't understand the signal I'm giving him. He's a serious pain in the ass. My eyes narrow, the more tired of his bullshit I become until he finally does what I ask.

"I don't know about y'all, but I'm starving. Lunch? Hellcat, why don't you come help me whip up some of that fancy Mexican cuisine?" Axel tilts his head for her to follow and I jerk mine back in appreciation. Sometimes he's not a complete dumbass.

When they're in the kitchen and out of earshot, I lean in to ask, "Were you able to get what I need?"

He nods. "You'd be amazed how easily people talk with the right motivation. He was executed with a single gunshot to the head and had the word '*venganza*' carved into his chest."

"Shit." Zane grinds his teeth so hard I'm surprised they haven't turned to dust. He knows this doesn't bode well for us.

"That mean somethin' to you?" Carl's eyebrows pinch together.

"It does. It's Spanish for 'revenge' or for all intents and purposes, payback." Which means it was a message for me, not Charlee. If that's the case, why don't I feel a sense of relief at hearing this?

"Fuck." Carl's shoulders tense. "That means someone has cottoned on to what you're doin'. Maybe you should quit now? No one would blame you if you did." His black eyes shoot to Charlee and back to me.

"Not an option." My voice brooks no further argument. What happened sucks and has fucked with what I had planned, but it's not stopping me. I've come too far to give up now. It's a good thing I'm adaptable.

"Ash, man, think ab—"

"I appreciate the concern, brother, but it's not happening."

His mouth closes. He knows there's no use trying to persuade me because once my mind's made up, there's no changing it. "You've got another problem."

"What's that?" Something about the way his voice lowers has my teeth on edge.

"Cops have been asking around about you. Sooner or later that shit's gonna get back to the wrong people."

"Rosenberg won't find me."

"The district attorney?" A vein in the side of Zane's neck pulses.

"Not talkin' about him. Worse. Word on the street is Governor Loren's daughter was seen hitting up a club with your boy over there." He tilts his head in Axel's direction. "If I found this out, you know damn well they'll be gunning for all three of your asses."

"It's nothing I can't manage," I assure my brother and then turn my attention to Carl. "You let me worry about all that."

"How? By doing somethin' stupid and gettin' caught? This isn't gonna just go away, man. You get locked up again I won't be in there to have your back. They'd eat white boys like your brothers for breakfast and you fucking know it." Carl crosses his arms over his chest and eyes me like some dumb motherfucker who was born yesterday. He's beginning to piss me off.

"I said I'll handle it." My fist comes down on the table hard enough to get my point across, but not hard enough to draw Charlee's attention.

He puts his hands up in surrender before dropping them back to his sides. "Okay, I'll let it go." He points a finger in my face. "But you get any blowback, I was never fuckin' involved."

"Fair enough."

"Besides, looks to me like you might have your hands full of other things right now anyhow." He lights a cigarette and leans back in his chair as his lips curl into a wide grin.

"Leave it alone, brother."

He shakes his head, not affected in the least by my anger. Typical Carl. Which is good because it makes what I have to ask him next that much easier.

"I need another favor."

"Oh, really?"

"We're going hunting and I don't want to leave her here alone. After what happened I have a bad feeling."

"Sure, I can babysit. I'm great at watching. The kiddies love me." He winks. There's no mistaking what he's getting at and I squash that shit down fast.

"You lay so much as a finger on her, I'll cut it off and make you choke on it."

He doesn't say another word and I don't wait for him to. He knows better. Conversation over, I go back to watching Charlee. There's a light on her face that wasn't there before, and a slight pang of guilt hits me. She looks so happy and carefree as she and Axel fix lunch, making me feel like a bastard. It's my fault she's in the middle of this in the first place. Hopefully she'll forgive me for leaving her behind.

Her soft laughter fills the air, hitting me right in the center of my chest. Seeing her stand in my kitchen like she belongs there has my insides doing weird shit. This girl is something else and when this bullshit is all over, I'm not sure what I'm going to do because if there's one thing I do know, it's that my brothers are right. I can't let her go.

After lunch, we end up shooting the shit for a few hours and just hanging out. Things are pretty low key. It isn't until later in the night when we're grabbing our jackets that Charlee realizes something's up.

"What's going on?" Her green eyes are wide and on alert as she watches Axel and Zane walk out the front door. She's not dumb. Lying will only make it worse, so I go with abrupt honesty.

"We're leaving. We'll be back." I'm not giving her more information than that or she'll try to stop me.

"Like hell, you're leaving me behind." Her hands go to her hips and I brace for the shit storm that's coming. Judging by the red staining her cheeks, it's going to be an all-out war.

"This isn't up for discussion, Charlee."

"Don't you 'Charlee' me." She jabs the tip of her finger into my chest. "I'm coming with you and you can't stop me."

"You're staying here where it's safe. Can you behave while I'm gone?"

"No. I won't."

"Wrong answer." I dip forward and dig my shoulder into her hip as I lift her off the floor. She should know that if she throws down the gauntlet, I'm gonna win.

"Put me down, Asher!" Her tiny fists pound into my back, but I don't even feel it. It doesn't stop her from trying, though. "I swear I'm going to kick your ass if you don't."

"Be good while I'm gone, Princess." I slam the door and lock her inside, but it isn't long before her door becomes the substitute for my back. Those fists of hers are doing their damnedest to break through. I tap down the slight pang of guilt creeping into my gut and face

Carl. "She doesn't come out until we're long gone and you don't let her out of your sight. She's too stubborn not to hotwire your car and go out looking for us."

A horn honks from outside, letting me know my brothers are as anxious as I am to get this done.

Carl leans against the wall next to her door, as she continues to pound on it. "She won't leave this house. You have my word on that."

With that, I nod and walk out the door. The only thing playing in the back of my mind is that I'm almost done. One more and it'll all be over. I should have known it wouldn't be that easy, though. Nothing ever is.

CHAPTER TWENTY-NINE

ASHER

I WATCH MY BROTHERS STRING up Mateo like he's a piñata. Before the night is through, he'll be spilling something sweeter than candy—his blood. When we found him, he was still in the parking lot of Viper's Den. He never even made it past his car before we were on him and had him hog-tied and knocked out in the back of the van. Lucky for us, he's stayed out the entire thirty-minute drive to the farm.

"How much does this fucker weigh?" Axel grunts as he and Zane tie him to the post.

"Quit whining like a little bitch and hold him up." Zane smacks him upside the head and continues winding the rope around Mateo's body.

"Whatever, man." Axel kneels down to gain a better hold, but his feet slip against the mud, causing Mateo to fall forward.

"Hold him up," Zane growls.

"Easy for you to say. You're not the one with a face full of dick." Axel grunts and pushes Mateo back up. "Good thing it's small."

Zane shoots me a look, asking for patience, and I shrug. My lips twitch, but I fight the urge to smile. I've missed my brothers. Even if circumstances have changed between us, things are still the same in many ways.

Axel pours a bucket of cold water on the prick's face. "Wakey, wakey!"

Mateo comes to and struggles against the wooden post.

I watch him for a few beats before I make myself known, stepping out of the shadows into his line of sight. "You ain't going anywhere." Zane made sure of that.

Mateo's head twists in the direction of my voice. It takes a second for him to register what he's seeing, but when he does, his face hardens. "I should have known it was you. You always did hit like a pussy." A small breeze blows past, causing him to shiver.

"Cold?" Axel laughs and leans against the wooden railing of the fence.

Mateo looks down. "Where the fuck are my clothes?" His black eyes glare at me.

"You won't need them where you're going." Zane's right. This piece of shit won't need a fucking thing where I'm sending him.

Pigs squeal from the pen next to us, drawing Mateo's attention. "Ain't that fitting?" His gaze swings back to me. "I'm surrounded by pigs."

"They haven't eaten in a couple of days, so they're nice and hungry," Zane taunts.

I enjoy the brief flicker of fear in Mateo's eyes before I speak. "Give me a name, Mateo." My patience is running thin. I don't want to stay out here freezing my balls off all fucking night. After all, I still have a foul-mouthed little vixen to punish.

"Fuck you, *hijo de puta*." The asshole spits at my feet.

"You ain't very smart, are ya?" Axel laughs from behind me.

Annoyed, I pull out my knife and press the tip against his neck with one hand while the other squeezes his cheeks. "Let's try this again. Give me a name or I'm going to gut you and strangle you with your own intestines."

Mateo grunts from the pressure, but he isn't done fighting yet.

"You're so fucking dumb you can't even see what's right in front of you—what's been right in front of your face this whole fucking time."

"Why don't you explain it to me then?" My fingers increase their pressure, digging deeper into the sides of his face, warning him that I'm not fucking around. When he still doesn't give me what I want, I punch him in the face until I can hear his bones cracking underneath my knuckles with each blow. I raise my fist ready to strike again when a pair of hands grab me from behind.

"Enough, Ash. He can't talk if he's dead." Zane squeezes my shoulder before releasing his grip and handing me my knife from the ground. He walks around to stand behind Mateo, waiting. Axel mirrors his movement. Without words, my brothers are letting me know they have my back.

My body is racing with adrenaline and itching for more, but Zane's words sink in. I suck in a few deep gulps of air to steady my breathing and glare at Mateo. Blood seeps out of his mouth and drips down his chin. One of his eyes is starting to swell shut and I feel a sense of peace wash over me at the sight of every wound I've inflicted, but his suffering has only just begun.

I trail the knife down the bridge of his nose, down his neck, stopping at his chest. With a bit of pressure, I push the tip in until a trickle of blood seeps out. "Spill your guts or I will."

"Fuck you, *pendejo*." Mateo grunts, but never releases my gaze. "I'm dead either way."

"Tell me what I want to know."

"Go to Hell," he spits back.

"I was there for six years!" My lungs burn with rage, begging me to unleash the monster from its cage. This asshole will pay. "And now it's your turn." I kneel down in front of him and he laughs.

"What? You gonna suck my dick, *Cabrón*? I bet they taught you how to take cock like a good little bitch in prison." Sweat drips down his forehead as the muscles in his jaw clench. I'd blame the Georgia humidity, but I can see the fear behind his eyes. It's clear as day now, and I'm going to feed off of every last bit of it.

I take his dick in my hand and squeeze as hard as I can. His screams flood my veins like a drug. It's not enough. I need a bigger fix. When I'm through, he will know what true fear is. "This is not even close to the pain Lauren felt when you attacked her, you sick piece of shit." I bring my knife down, slicing into his flesh. Blood fills my hands as it leaves his body and I want to bathe in it.

Mateo tilts his head back and screams, but Zane pushes his head back down, forcing him to watch me slice him apart. "Keep your eyes open. You don't want to miss this." Mateo's screams echo against the night sky as I continue to carve away at him until his severed dick is in my hands. When I look up, I find immense pleasure in the agony written across his face.

"That has to fucking hurt." Axel winces, but he makes no move to intervene, which is smart. I'm so far gone there's no way I'm stopping. Even if I wanted to, I couldn't. I've let my monster out to play and he wants more than his pound of flesh. He wants it all.

"Fuck you," Mateo wheezes like a dying animal. His body is going limp from blood loss, but I'm not done with him yet.

I toss what's left of his dick onto the ground at his feet before standing to watch the color drain from his face. He deserves every bit of pain I inflict. I want nothing more than to spend the night torturing him, but I'm on a schedule. I tilt my chin in Zane's direction and he cuts Mateo down, as Axel opens the pen door. Mateo falls to the ground in a limp heap, and the pigs rush in. They waste no time heading devouring the treat I just served up for them.

"The only fucked one here is you." A smirk spreads across my face as I watch them swarm him, attacking every piece of flesh they can.

"Those fuckers sure can eat." Axel watches for a brief second before following us out and closing the pen behind him.

I light up a cigarette as we head back to the truck. The sounds of Mateo's screams hum like music to my ears the entire way.

When we reach the truck, Zane throws his shit in the back and paces. "What the fuck did he mean by that?"

"Yeah. If it ain't Diego, then who the fuck would do this?" Axel's face pinches tight. He's not liking this one bit, and I have to admit neither am I.

"I don't know." I blow out a cloud of smoke and hold both of my brother's stares. "But, we're going to find out." Something in my gut tells me Mateo wasn't lying and the one responsible is even closer than I thought. That thought is like a swift kick in the nuts, but no matter. I'll be coming for them, whoever they are.

CHAPTER
THIRTY

CHARLEE

MY FIST IS RAISED READY to bang on the door again when it flies open. I jump back and glare at my babysitter. Anger pulses through my veins like a poison, which is all directed at Carl. He may not have locked me in here, but he's guilty by association.

His dark eyes take in my flushed state as he leans against the doorjamb with what appears to be a shirt in his hands. "You calmed down enough to come out?"

I put my hands on my hips and glare at him. "What do you think? He locked me in my room again, like I'm a damn child."

He doesn't even blink an eye at my attitude. "I'll let you come downstairs if you promise to behave. That means no tryin' to fight me and no sneakin' out to steal my car." He runs his hand through his dreads as he waits for my answer.

"Sure." Adrenaline floods my system as I prepare to make a run for it. It takes everything I have to keep my voice calm and steady so he doesn't catch on to my plan, but I must answer too fast because his dark eyes narrow at me.

"Take off your pants, Charlee."

My body goes ramrod straight at his request. That's not fucking happening. "Excuse me? I will do no such thing. Besides, my tank top is too short and there's no way in hell I'm walking around you in just my underwear."

"You don't have nothin' I haven't seen before." He snickers.

My hands ball into fists and I'm seconds away from junk punching the asshole.

"Chill the fuck out, woman. I'm not gonna try anything. Asher would have my balls in a vise, and I happen to like them where they are, thank you very much. He also let me know what you did to Axel." Heat creeps into my cheeks when he brings that up. "Without pants, you can't get very far now, can ya?" Bastard is smart, but I'm smarter.

I don't dignify his remark with an answer. Instead, I just stand there glaring back at him in a silent dare to make me.

A few seconds tick by and then he sighs. "Come on, Charlee. I'm doin' my boy a solid here. Can you work with me a little bit? I really don't want to have to tie your sweet ass up, but you fuck me on this, and I'll have no other choice."

"I won't. You have my word that I'll behave." He doesn't appear to believe me in the slightest, which is smart because I never do what I'm told.

"Glad to hear it." He tosses the shirt he's holding in my face and I catch it before it can smack me. "Put this on."

"You going to turn around then?" I give in because if I change at least he'll think I'm cooperating. Like a damn t-shirt can stop me from doing what I want.

"So you can knock me on the back of the head? I don't think so." He presses his weight harder against the wall and crosses his arms over his chest.

I fight back the retort that's brewing on the tip of my tongue and turn my back to him.

Asshole!

I change as best I can without showing him anything. Whiskey and tobacco float off the fabric and I know I'm wearing yet another one of Asher's shirts. Even though I'm pissed at the asshole, I can't deny I love the smell of him.

"Meet me in the livin' room." He pushes off the wall and heads down the hall to the stairs. He gets about halfway and stops to call out, "Want a beer, Charlee?"

"No. I'll take a shot of whiskey, though." Anything to make him take longer and give me a chance to sneak out.

"Sure thing." He nods, and I listen to his footsteps until they disappear into the distance.

Once I'm sure he's far enough away, I creep down the stairs as quietly as I can until I reach the front door. My head whips around, scanning the room, but Carl's still busy fixing our drinks in the kitchen. I hold my breath and twist the knob, hoping it doesn't make a sound. Every second feels like an eternity as I struggle with the damn thing. A beat later it gives and the knowledge that I'm almost free is bittersweet. The minute the door opens, I make a move to run for it, but a deep voice scares the shit out of me.

"Don't even think about it, Charlee. I'll be on you before you can make it to the door and then you'll spend the rest of the night mad I hog-tied your ass. Not to mention, you almost ended up as some coyote's dinner last time."

"Ugh!" Foiled, I storm off into the living room and plop down on the couch without sparing him a glance.

Carl strolls into the living room with a beer in one hand and my shot in the other. He stops in front of me and holds it out like I didn't just throw a temper tantrum. "Here. This should help you feel better."

"Thanks." I toss back the whiskey in one go and let the warmth of it burn through me as I watch Carl sit in the recliner across from the couch and pick up the remote.

"Want to watch a little TV?" When I don't spare him an answer, he presses. "Charlee?"

"Fine." I drop the shot glass on the table and glare up at the flat screen. "Put on whatever you want then."

A corner of his mouth lifts into a slight grin. "Asher's so fucked."

I open my mouth to snap back, but the opening credits on the

TV stop me. "Lucifer?" My eyebrows quirk up as I shoot him a look. Never thought that he would pick that, but it's one of my favorite shows, so he'll get no complaints from me.

"The devil you know and all that, right?" He shrugs and takes a swig of his beer.

"Right, and I'm sure Chloe Decker isn't hard to look at." There's no controlling my eye roll.

"She's a hot piece, but it's Linda who really does it for me."

"The doctor?" I wasn't expecting that answer. I guess Carl is full of surprises tonight.

"She's hot and smart. That's a fantasy come to life right there." He points the tip of the amber bottle in my direction as his dark eyes glisten. "Judging by your face that's not who you were expecting me to say. You telling me you're not a fan of hers?"

"She's okay, I guess."

"Let me guess. You got a hard-on for Lucifer?"

"He's hot, but I'm more of a Mazikeen fan." I sink deeper into the couch and sigh. It's obvious I'm not going anywhere, so I might as well get comfortable, and I won't admit it to Carl but wearing this t-shirt was a good call.

"Figures you'd pick the badass brunette." He never takes his eyes off of me as he props his feet up on the coffee table and lounges back against the leather.

I shake my head and laugh. At least if I'm going to be stuck here, I'm in good company. While the opening credits play, I take the opportunity to really study him. He's definitely good looking. His white shirt is a compliment to his dark skin. Much like Asher, his muscular arms are covered in tattoos. There's one of a snake that winds up his neck and disappears just under his jawline. There's a rough edge to him that's all too familiar.

"Asher met you in prison, didn't he?" My fingers toy with the hem of my shirt.

The muscles of his throat bob as he takes his time swallowing another sip of his beer, no doubt to stall answering my question. "He did."

"Interesting." My teeth dig into my bottom lip to keep from pressing him for more information. It's not my place to ask.

"I can see the wheels spinnin' in that pretty head of yours. I'm not gonna spew a bunch of bullshit to you and proclaim my innocence. I was guilty as fuck for what I did, and I'd do it again."

"What were you in for?"

"Which time?" He snorts.

"Umm."

"Relax, Charlee. I'm messin' with you." He chuckles. "I guess you could say I was a product of my environment. Started with stupid shit like boostin' cars and worked my way up from there."

"You ever kill anyone?" I don't know what's wrong with me. It's like I have diarrhea of the mouth and I can't stop talking.

"Have you?" He turns my question back around on me.

"Sorry. Stupid question."

"It's fine. Let's just say I was young and stupid, and leave it at that."

"Fair enough." Our conversation dies as I nod and glance back up to the TV. I cheer every time Maze kicks some punk's ass and Carl just laughs at me. We lose track of time as we're sucked into episode after episode.

While we're watching the last episode of season one, the front door bursts open and in strolls Asher. He doesn't even spare us a glance as he rushes up the stairs into his room. Carl calls out to him a couple of times, but it's like he's lost in a trance and never answers.

"He'll be all right. He just needs a minute to get his head on straight." Zane walks into the living room and leans against the nearby wall.

Axel comes in behind him, and when his blue eyes glance up at the TV, he grins. "This show is awesome. Linda is the shit."

Carl gives me a knowing look before he stands up and makes his way to the door. "Well, since y'all are back in one piece, I'm gonna head back home."

"I'll walk you out." Zane follows him outside with Axel trailing behind them. I get the feeling they want to talk in private, which is fine.

I have a bone to pick with the one upstairs because he has another thing coming if he thinks I'm not going to be giving him any shit after what he pulled tonight. All anger disappears when I get to his room, though.

Asher's covered in blood. He looks like a nightmare come to life, one I should be running away from, but sometimes a little danger is good for the soul.

CHAPTER THIRTY-ONE

ASHER

I TURN ON THE SHOWER before moving to the sink. The reflection staring back at me from the mirror is one I don't recognize anymore. Blood stains my hands and face, but a grin breaks free as I hear Mateo's screams begging for mercy. Mercy I didn't give. Mercy nobody gave to Lauren or our child. Justice was served tonight.

My hands begin to tremble as the earlier adrenaline rush wears off. I grip the sides of the cool porcelain, dirtying the pristine white with my sins. My heart pounds as I take slow, deep breaths. Every inch of my skin feels like a live wire ready to explode while I struggle to get the bastard's words out of my head. He could have just been talking shit, but something in my gut isn't convinced of that.

Movement off to the left catches my eye through the mirror, and as I twist around, my throat goes dry at the image before me. Charlee is standing there in my shirt and nothing else. All of the blood rushes straight to my dick at the sight.

"What are you doing in here?" My voice comes out rough and dry, like I've swallowed nails.

She crosses her arms over her chest and meets my stare head-on. "I saw you run up the stairs like your ass was on fire and wanted to check on you." Her head lifts and the second her green eyes meet mine, everything inside of me stills. This is the closest she's come to seeing me for what I truly am.

Dressed in black from head to toe, I look like the grim reaper ready to snuff out her last breath, but she isn't running. She moves forward until her toes are touching the tips of my boots. I watch, waiting for fear to take over, but her gaze remains steady and calm as she sees the blood on my hands.

"Are you hurt?" she asks.

"No." I shake my head and swallow the lump forming in my throat. If she only knew what I've done—that I'm no better than the man she called father—I don't think she'd be looking at me the same way.

The steam from the shower begins to swirl around us like a cloud of smoke, but my attention never strays from her. I'm standing here, exposed and raw. As much as I hate it, I still want her to see all of me, see the kind of man I am. And if she wants to run, I'll let her go this time. It'll gut me, but for her, I'll do it.

"Is that your blood?" Her green eyes narrow as she takes in more of my appearance.

"No." Seeing her in my clothes has my blood pumping so hard that I can't give any more than one-word answers.

A sigh escapes those plump lips as her arms slide down my chest to the bottom of my shirt, the touch of her fingers igniting a hunger deep inside of me, one that only she can sate. My mouth waters, wanting to taste every inch of her olive skin with my tongue. It's wreaking havoc on my insides, but I stay firmly rooted to my spot, enjoying her newfound boldness.

Fire burns behind her eyes as she gives a slight tug on the cotton. "I want to see you. All of you."

I raise my arms over my head, granting her permission without words. She whips my shirt off and drops her eyes down to the hard planes of my abs a second before she kneels down in front of me, her fingers working the fly of my jeans with record precision.

My fists clench as droplets of blood fall down onto the white tile floor, fighting the urge to rip my shirt off her petite body and fuck her senseless. Somehow, I resist. I'm curious to see what she'll do next.

She finishes undressing me until I'm standing there naked with my rock hard dick on display. Her teeth sink into her bottom lip as she takes in her fill. Color stains her cheeks and a devilish smirk spreads onto her face.

"What are you waiting for?" she whispers, looking up at me. "I'm yours for the taking."

Her words break through the last shred of self-control I've been holding onto. I grip the sides of her ass, slamming her up against me until she feels the hard ridge of my cock digging into her taut stomach. One of my hands comes up to cup the side of her face, marring her perfect olive skin with a blemish of red. My thumb traces along her pouty lips, coating them in the same sea of blood. She's tarnished with my sins and she's never looked hotter.

"You're fucking perfect."

Through hooded eyes, she watches, waiting. Her hands hang loosely at her sides as her tits push up against my chest with every panting breath she takes. Our bodies glisten with moisture from the humidity enveloping the room.

My hand slips down and cups between her legs. She lets out a small gasp and I waste no time taking what is mine. What will always be mine. My mouth attacks hers, swallowing her cries of pleasure as I stroke her clit through the fabric of her panties. I delve my tongue inside her mouth, teasing her in tandem with my fingers.

"More. I need more." She rocks up onto the balls of her feet, giving me better access. "Please."

My hand moves farther down between the lips of her pussy until I'm as far inside her as the flimsy material will allow. I curl my fingers and work them back and forth, watching her the entire time.

She throws her head back and digs her nails into my biceps. The harder she presses into my skin, the faster I move until her whole body is shaking from the orgasm wracking through her body.

"Holy shit." Her head rests against my shoulder as her body goes limp in my arms. She pants while her body shudders with tiny after-shocks, and it's the hottest thing I've ever seen.

"We're just getting started." I pull my fingers out from inside her and rip all of the clothes from her body in one quick motion before wrapping her legs around me and stepping inside the shower. The heat of her exposed core presses against me, taunting me like a dessert. One I need to taste.

I set her on her feet and kneel down between her legs. Water beats down on me as I wrap a leg over my shoulder and spread her lips apart with my thumbs. My tongue flicks out against her clit, playing her like a violin. Every stroke winds her body up tighter and tighter until she's ready to snap. She's so sensitive that it isn't long before I'm pulling another orgasm from her.

Watching her come apart has my dick ready to explode. My balls tighten at the thought of being inside her again. I stand and pin her back up against the tile wall. My hips thrust forward along her slit, coating my dick in her juices.

"Fuck me," she groans at the contact. "I need you to fuck me hard." It's a plea and one that will not go ignored.

"Hang onto me." Without warning, I slam into her hard and fast, the slick heat of her pussy surrounding me. It's tight and soft and feels like heaven. Her head falls back against the tile exposing the smooth planes of her neck. I lean forward and sink my teeth into the sensitive flesh.

"Oh God," she moans. The harder I sink my dick and teeth into her, the louder she becomes.

Each sound she makes has my pulse racing. I continue to thrust into her with a punishing pace until her walls contract around me, and squeeze, drawing the orgasm from my body. Every one of my muscles tenses as my cock twitches with my release, marking her from the inside out as mine.

Our hearts race in sync as a mixture of sweat and water coats my back. I press my forehead against hers, letting my breathing even out. A sense of calm washes over me as I continue to hold her against me. Amongst the chaos around me, she's become the very thing keeping me grounded.

Minutes pass before we're able to move again. I lift my head and my chest tightens at what I see. Face flushed, lips swollen—she's a perfect sight.

"That was…" She goes limp in my arms, unable to finish her thoughts. When she moves her head, I can't stop the grin that breaks free. The sight of my mark on her body isn't something I'll ever tire of seeing. My dick likes it, too, because he's already ready for round two.

"I'm not done fucking you, Princess." And fuck her I do, not stopping until we're both numb and sated.

After the shower, we made it to the bed for another round. We're now lying down underneath the sheets, each lost in our own thoughts.

A few more beats of silence pass before Charlee picks up the framed picture of Lauren from the nightstand, drawing my attention to her, and rubs a finger against the metal edges. "Tell me more about her?"

I grab a cigarette from the pack on the nightstand and light it up. After a long drag, I exhale and give her what she wants. "We were just kids when we met, but inseparable from the first day." A smile plays on my lips as memories of her flood my mind. "We were each other's first everything. Everyone said we were like a goddamn fairy-tale." I shake my head as the words taste like ash on my tongue. Some happy ending we got.

"She sounds perfect." There's no malice in her words, only understanding, and it's another reason my head is slowly starting to catch up with my heart when it comes to her.

"She was my rock, the one who got me through the academy. She'd teach kindergarten during the day and handle everything at home after work so I could keep up with my rigorous schedule there." I stop to take another drag from my cigarette, needing the nicotine rush to continue. "When…" Emotion claws at my throat like a knife, cutting off my voice. Six years and the pain hasn't faded one damn bit. It's just as fresh as the day it happened.

Charlee tightens the arm laying across my chest, anchoring me to the present. I clear my throat and force myself to go on.

"When we found out we were having a boy, she went to the store and bought every damn blue thing they had." I laugh to myself, remembering it like it was yesterday. My hand absently rubs against her naked back as I let the images fall, and instead of being overcome with the usual sadness, I'm feeling lighter, like a small weight's being lifted as I share my family, a part of my past with her.

She listens until I'm all talked out, never once showing me pity or seeing me as weak for failing to protect them. Her finger draws lazy circles over my chest as we lie in comfortable silence, letting everything I've said linger between us. Things feel like they're finally falling into place, but nothing is ever that easy.

CHAPTER THIRTY-TWO

CHARLEE

"MY FATHER MIGHT HAVE BEEN a lot of things, but he would never have hurt her or your unborn child." I know it down to my soul. My father had a rule about hurting women and children.

"I was there, Charlee. It was his men who carried out the orders —orders given by him." He snorts and I can sense the mood changing in the room.

I shake my head, undeterred by his anger. "No. He wouldn't have done that," I repeat with more conviction than before.

Asher shoves his legs into a pair of jeans and storms out of the room into the small office. I grip the sheet tighter against my chest and wonder if I should chase after him, but it isn't long before I hear his footsteps echo against the wooden floor. The rage behind his eyes the second he comes back in should frighten me, but I'm too focused on the manila folder in his hand to think about anything else.

He tosses the folder onto the bed in front of me and stands with his fists clenched at his sides. "This is what those bastards did to her and my unborn son."

Taking a deep breath, I flip open the folder. Dozens of pictures fall out and I'm not prepared for what I see. Tears pool in my eyes as my hand flies up to my mouth. Nausea churns in my stomach the longer I stare at the images. This is like something out of a horror movie. Blood is everywhere. From the carpet to the white comforter, it stains it all. The body of a woman with a very pregnant belly is lying limp on the bed with multiple stab wounds all over her chest.

"Oh my God. I'm so sorry, Asher." Bile inches its way up my throat. I can't imagine what he went through that night.

A muscle ticks in his jaw, but he doesn't move otherwise. Pain is etched onto every line of his face and my heart shatters into a million pieces for him.

I shift the folder onto my lap and another photograph slips out. This one is of two men. Two men I've seen hanging around. "I know them."

"Of course you do. They work for that piece of shit, Diego."

"No. They don't." I shake my head and do my best to ignore the insult about my father. Asher's anger is understandable, even though it's misplaced. "They work for Marco."

Asher's nostrils flare as he lets my words sink in. His head shakes back and forth so hard that I'm surprised he doesn't get whiplash. "No!" His body trembles as he loses all self-control. The next thing I know, he has me by the throat and slammed up against the nearest wall. My feet dangle as my toes barely graze the floor. It's not lost on me that I was in this exact position the first time we met.

"You're lying. Those are the bastards who killed her, and your father is the one who gave the order." His face dips so close to mine that I can feel the whisper soft touch of his lips against mine as he speaks. Cold air hits my naked body, but I don't break eye contact.

My heart hammers against my chest as he stares at me with those hard, dead eyes, but I swallow down my emotions and keep trying to reach him. "I'm not. I know all of my father's men and they are not his. I've seen Marco hanging around them, but my dad would never give those two the time of day." Every word comes out slow and careful, a silent plea for him to hear me, hear the truth in my words.

The hair from his arm tickles my nipple with every breath I take as I wait to see how this plays out.

"No." Asher's hanging on by a thread, but he needs to believe me. He's hated the wrong man all this time. His fingers flex deeper into the sides of my neck as he struggles to come to terms with the bomb I've just dropped on him. The fist of his other hand comes up and punches the wall next to my head, going right through it.

My body flinches, but I don't move otherwise. He won't hurt me. Not like that. At least not anymore.

"What happened to your family was awful and nobody should ever have to go through that, but it's the truth. I swear to you on my life."

His slow shallow breathing is the only sound that stretches between us as his mind works through and processes things. Tension leaves his body and the second it does, the hand around my throat goes lax, but I don't move.

"Fuck!" He collapses onto the floor and puts his hands on top of his head. Blood seeps out of his split knuckles and drips down his wrists, but he doesn't appear to feel it.

I kneel down next to him and take his bloody hand in mine. Words aren't necessary. Silence speaks louder than they ever could. I let him mourn. Mourn for the loss of his family, for the loss of an innocent child. And for the loss of a life he never got to live.

"It's okay, Asher."

"No, it's not. Nothing about this is okay. I was so sure it was him and—and I took you." He swallows and shakes his head. "I'm no fucking better than they are."

Seeing his pain is like a knife to my chest. He may have started out as the devil, as the one who tried to ruin me, but he's become my savior. I take his face in my hands and force him to meet my gaze. "Listen to me. You are nothing like them. Do you hear me? Nothing. They did this. Not you. Them. If anybody should be feeling guilty, it's the monsters who killed your family. You're a good man, Asher Savage, and I'll be damned if I let you think otherwise."

His eyes gloss over as his hands grab the sides of my face. He presses his lips against mine and devours my mouth, hard and demanding. He's taking, but he's also giving at the same time. All of his emotions, words unspoken, are being poured out into this kiss. My heart soars with every touch of his tongue. There's no doubt of his feelings for me. When he pulls back, my lips feel swollen and bruised, and beg for more.

He presses his forehead against mine and sighs. "You're mine, Charlee. I'm not giving you up without a fight."

Our heavy breathing fills the room as I relish his warmth. My hands rub the back of his neck, letting this moment—our moment—linger. Then his phone rings, shattering the silence.

Asher's eyes narrow as he takes it out of his pocket and looks at the number. He holds it up to his ear and lets out a gruff, "Yeah?" His body tenses next to mine. "I'm on my way." Just as quickly as he ends the call, he stands, and I follow. Without a word, he kisses me on the top of the head and toward the open door.

"Where are you going?"

"To make this right, for both of us." He spins on his heels and storms out the door.

"Wait!" I move to chase after him, but the cold air hitting my naked body stops me. In record time, I'm dressed in yoga pants and a tank top, and my bare feet are slapping down the stairs, but it's too late. The second I make it out the door I see the taillights of the truck disappearing through the trees and three figures sitting inside the cab.

"Damn it!" I'm left standing there alone, wondering what the hell he's going to do.

Movement from the shadows next to me catches my eye and I turn in time to make contact with a fist. The force of it knocks me to the ground. Pain explodes along the side of my head as my vision swims in and out of focus.

"Missed you, *Chiquita*," is all I hear before my eyes close and everything goes black.

CHAPTER THIRTY-THREE

ASHER

I T KILLED ME TO SEE Charlee running after me in the rearview mirror, but I know she's safer at the house than anywhere else. I can't risk anything happening to her. She's become too important for me to risk.

"What did Carl say?" Axel fidgets next to me. Both, he and Zane are nervous as fuck since I told them we needed to go without much of an explanation.

"That he found something—something that was too important to say over the phone." I flick the ash of my cigarette out the window and keep a steady grip on the steering wheel with my other hand. For a brief second, I toy with keeping the information Charlee shared to myself, but I know better. My brothers are as knee deep in this shit as I am. "Charlee said something earlier, something that has put a serious fucking wrench in our plans."

"What did she say?" Zane's attention turns from the window and onto me.

I play with the butt of my cigarette a few times before I manage to get the words out. "The hit wasn't ordered by Diego."

"Then who the hell was it?" I see Axel grind his teeth out of the corner of my eyes.

"Marco." The second I say his name, the air in the cab becomes thick with tension.

"Are you fucking serious?" Zane's voice deepens as he puts together the same thing I did the second Charlee told me. "This means Marco has to have another partner because there's no way he'd be able to keep it from Diego on his own."

"It does." I take my eyes off the road for a quick second to nod in his direction.

"Fuck me." Axel runs a hand down his face. "This is bad. This is really fucking bad. What are we gonna do?"

"Let's see what Carl says first and go from there." I shrug off his concern, but inside, I'm a ball of chaos. I'm not sure what the hell this all means, and I have a bad feeling things are about to get worse before they get better.

The rest of the thirty-minute drive is done in silence. We're each left to stew in our own thoughts. Things are fucked up, but we've come too far to quit now. A few minutes later we pull up to Carl's house and a strange sense of unease hits me the second I park in the driveway. I feel it down to my bones. It's a feeling that never failed to keep my ass safe in prison.

"What's wrong?" Zane asks the second I kill the ignition.

"Something's not right."

"What do you mean?" Axel glances around the front yard looking for anything to back up my words.

"I don't know. I just feel it in my gut. We need to watch our asses. Zane, you cover the rear and Axel, you keep your eyes open." I exit the truck but leave the door open. The last thing we want to do is attract any more attention if we can help it.

Both of my brothers nod and slowly creep out of the truck, careful not to make a sound. They pull out their guns and flank me the whole way up the front porch. When we reach the door, my jaw clenches. It's slightly open and the wood of the doorjamb is splintered. A vein throbs in my temple as a flashback of the night Lauren was killed threatens to break free, but I do my best to breathe through it and stay focused. I can't afford any mistakes. Not right now.

The toe of my boot nudges the door open and we slip through without making a sound. Nothing appears to be out of place in the living room, so we ease our way farther inside to the back of the house where the kitchen is. The second we round the corner, everything turns to shit.

Glass and broken dishes litter the dingy linoleum floor. Cupboards are broken and blood is splattered across the white cabinets. Carl's body is lying limp in the middle of his kitchen. Blood is all over him and pooling on the floor around his body.

I rush over to him and kneel down to check his pulse. It's faint, but it's there nonetheless. "Carl? Who the fuck did this?" My hands roam over his body, assessing his injuries. He has several knife wounds to his abdomen and chest. Whoever did this carved him up like a fucking turkey.

"Ash…I'm…so..rr..y…" he wheezes out as blood spews out of his mouth and down the side of his face.

"Hang on, brother." I rip off my shirt and use it to stop some of the blood flow. Zane and Axel rush to my side and do their best to help me.

"That's a lot of blood, Ash." Axel presses his shirt into Carl's side, the gray material turning crimson.

"We need to stop it." I refuse to believe this is the end for him.

"I'm sorry, Ash. We can't. He's lost too much blood." Zane's mouth presses together into a firm line as he shakes his head.

I glance up at my friend's face and see that he's fading fast. His fingers twitch and I grip his hand to let him know he's not going to die alone. Something hard hits my hand, but I'm not taking my eyes off of Carl. Not until he takes his last breath.

"I'm not going to let them get away with this. I promise you that."

Carl wheezes a few more times before his chest stops moving and the sound fades away. His eyes stare unblinking as the life leaves his body.

"Rest in peace, my brother." I close his eyes and bow my head, allowing him that last respect. My hand squeezes his one last time, and when I let go, I see what he was holding.

"Goddamn it!" A vein throbs in my forehead as I see red.

"What's wrong?"

I glance up to answer Zane when a flashing light from underneath one of the kitchen chairs catches my eye. Things have just gone from bad to worse.

"Outside, now!" I grab my brothers by the arms and haul ass out the back door. We only get a few feet away from the house before the blast hits. The force of it knocks us forward a good distance. We land in the grass, face first. Hands cradle our heads to protect our faces from flying debris. When things settle, I roll onto my feet and help my brothers up.

"They knew we were coming." Axel coughs and brushes himself off.

Images of dark hair and green eyes flood my mind, and heaviness settles into my gut like a lead weight. This is not fucking good.

"They did."

"How?" Zane pulls his eyebrows together.

"This." I slap the badge in Zane's hand.

Axel's eyes narrow as he takes in what I'm holding. "Is that what I think it is?"

"It is." I swallow down the bile of betrayal building in my throat. "I should have figured this shit out sooner. If I did, I could have…" My words get lodged in my throat.

"Don't go there, brother. It's not your fault." Zane's words do nothing to stop the ache that spreads across my chest.

"But, it is. It was my case that brought them to my house that night. They're dead because of me. Because I failed to protect them." The words feel like acid on my tongue, but it doesn't make them any less true.

"You can't shoulder the blame for this. It's on those fuckers who put the bullet in Lauren. Axel and I know it. And the fuckers will get everything that's coming to them, in spades."

"Damn right they will." Axel nods. I've never seen him so pissed.

This situation is more fucked than I could have ever thought. "We have to get back to the house, now!" I race to the truck with my brothers close behind. My foot hits the gas and I gun it toward Charlee, my heart in my throat the entire time.

I know something's wrong the second we pull up to the door and she doesn't run out to greet me. My feet tear up the gravel and into the house the second I kill the engine and everything is quiet. Too fucking quiet.

"Charlee?" I call out for her, hoping that my instincts are wrong. Silence answers me back. I run through the entire house, but come up empty. This can't be happening.

The sound of my phone ringing cuts through the empty house like a knife. When I pull it out and see Carl's number, my teeth grind together. I press the answer button and hold it up to my ear. "You're fucking dead."

A laugh—one that I haven't heard in six years—echoes through the phone's speaker. "I see you got my message."

"If you hurt her, I'm going to make you fucking suffer before I kill you." My throat burns with every word I speak, but I somehow manage to keep my shit together.

"She's too pretty for that. And besides, Marco has plans for her." The way he's referring to Charlee like she's a toy has my fists aching to break his neck.

"Don't you fucking touch her."

"Meet me at Viper's Den. Her safety depends on you, partner." The call goes dead before I can ask to hear her voice, and the line of sanity I've been straddling fades away.

They've taken enough from me. I'm bringing hell to their front door. And not a single one of them will survive this massacre when I'm through.

CHAPTER THIRTY-FOUR

CHARLEE

C OOL FINGERS RUN ALONG MY face, and when I open my eyes, a pair of familiar blue ones are staring back at me. "Kelsey?"

"Oh, thank god." Kelsey sighs and rubs away her streaked mascara. Her red hair is a knotted mess as it hangs down her back. "I thought they killed you." She leans back and helps me to a sitting position.

A sudden jolt of pain explodes along the back of my head the second I do. It feels like it's being split in half. My hands cradle around it only to find a huge lump that's tender to the touch.

I breathe through the pain and focus on Kelsey. Other than a split lip and a huge bruise on her cheek, she appears to be fine, but I know better than anyone some scars can't be seen. "Are you okay?"

"I'm so stupid." She sniffles and shakes her head. "I was pissed at Shawn—well, I guess the bastard's name is really Axel—for being another dick, so I went out to Orphic to get over him. I'm so stupid." I make a mental note to cut off Axel's balls for hurting my friend if I get out of here alive, but let her continue. "I didn't even make it through the door before they grabbed me and shoved me in a van, and I woke up here. Not before I could take a bite out of one of them, though."

"Where are we?" A sinking feeling hits me at her words.

"Viper's Den."

"The strip club?"

She nods. "They own it."

Shit. "Look at me, Kelsey. We'll get out of here. We will." I glance around the room to form a plan, but other than the door, there's no other way out of this room. We're basically sitting ducks unless I can figure out an escape. All thoughts of getting out of here die when the door opens.

Marco stands in the doorway with his arms folded across his chest. The grease on his dark hair shines underneath the fluorescent lighting, but it's his dark eyes that make everything inside of me still. They're lifeless and cold.

I hold my head high and look him in the eye. He will not intimidate me. "You murdered my dad. You're a sick bastard."

His lips spread into a smile, one that doesn't reach the rest of his face, and the unease I feel inside grows. "You should be more worried about yourself, *Chiquita*."

"You don't scare me." Despite all my bravado, my spine stiffens at his words.

"I should. I'm in charge now and *tu papá* can't protect you from me anymore." He uncrosses his arms and closes the distance between us until he's kneeling down in front of me. The scent of his cologne lingers in the air like a plague, sucking all the oxygen out if the room. I'm drowning in the stench of it.

Another set of footsteps enters the room. It isn't until he speaks again that I know things are about to get worse. Much worse.

"Take her out front and close the door," he calls over his shoulder, never taking his eyes off of mine.

A bald guy with a bite mark on his face grabs Kelsey from behind and shoves her in the direction of the open doorway.

"Leave her alone, you son of a bitch." Kelsey jerks against his grip and shouts the whole way out of the room.

The sound of the door latching closed seals my fate and I'm left alone, at the mercy of the devil.

"You're all mine now, Charlee." Marco leans in so close I can smell the tequila on his breath. It's bitter and deadly, nothing like the sweet scent of whiskey I've come to love. His finger grazes my cheek and I flinch at the contact. This only angers him further. He grabs me by the nape of the neck and forces me to look him in the eye. "Mine."

"I will never be yours."

"I warned you about that mouth of yours, *Chiquita*." His words are a huge contrast to his soothing tone. The tip of his nose trails along the side of my face and down to my neck where he sniffs me like I'm a fucking dog. "You smell like *him*." He leans back and grabs the sides of my face. "Did you let him fuck you?" His fingers dig deeper into my cheeks the longer I'm silent. "Answer me, Charlee!"

I jump at the sharpness of his tone but don't cower. It's not in my nature. My voice comes out smooth and controlled as I keep eye contact. "Yes! Several times."

The attack happens so fast that I don't realize I've been hit until I feel the pain. One second he's talking and the next his hand connects with the side of my face. It's a slow burn as the sting spreads across the rest of my cheek.

He fists my hair in a tight grip and yanks me up to my feet and against his chest. He pulls my head back to an uncomfortable angle and glares at me. "Tell me, *Chiquita*, did you enjoy spreading your legs for him? Being his whore? Because you won't enjoy anything I do to you, ever. And that's a fucking promise."

"Fuck you!" I spit back.

He lets out a hollow laugh before he slaps me across the face so hard I see stars. I'm knocked to the ground, trying to regain my balance, but he's not done punishing me. "I promise you'll be begging for death when I'm done with you." He kicks his foot into my stomach, knocking the wind out of me. I cough and fight back the urge to vomit as he does this a few more times. The only death I'll be begging for is his.

Just when I think he's done, he climbs on top of me and forces himself between my legs. I know what his intentions are, but I'll be damned if I let this fucker have any part of me. My body thrashes and fights against him with everything I have. I attempt to use one of the moves Asher taught me, but he's ready for it and blocks every single one. I do manage to scratch the side of his face, leaving a bloody trail of claw marks in my path. My lips twist into a deviant smile as I feel chunks of skin gather underneath my fingernails.

"I like it when you fight me. It gets me hard as fuck." He grinds against me, digging his erection into me. His hands roam over my body, gripping and squeezing every inch of my flesh in a bruising grip.

I spit in the fucker's face as tears threaten to spill, but I suck them back. This piece of shit won't get anything else from me.

A hollow laugh escapes him as I brace for another hit, but it doesn't come. He licks the side of my face and grunts. "Now, you smell like me."

I take advantage of this new position and slam my head forward into his. It hurts like a mother, but seeing the pain I've inflicted on him gives me some sense of satisfaction.

"You're going to regret that, *Chiquita*." His fingers go to the button of my jeans, playing along the edge of my waistband in slow circles. The bastard's torturing me with what comes next.

The sound of the door opening has my insides screaming in relief. All I can see from where I'm lying on the floor is a pair of men's dress shoes. "What the fuck are you doing, *Pendejo*?"

"Leave." Marco increases the pressure on my wrists and digs his groin against mine even harder, causing a grunt of disgust to leave me.

"No time. Asher's on his way and I need her in one piece. You can fuck her all you want after we kill him." The door shuts behind the stranger, leaving me at the mercy of this deranged fuck once again.

Marco yanks me to my feet and adjusts himself. I have just enough time to right my clothes before he grabs me by the arm and presses the barrel of his gun to my head. "Behave and I won't punish you too hard, *Chiquita*."

I'm dragged down a set of stairs and on to the main dance floor of the club. My eyes dart around the room looking for any signs of Kelsey, and when I find her, my body releases some of its tension. She's sitting next to the same bald guy who took her out of the room, and other than the bruises from earlier and a gag in her mouth, she appears to be fine, but the fear behind her blue eyes clutches at my heart. I need to get us out of here alive.

"Keep moving." Marco pushes me forward to the table next to Kelsey, but as we pass the stage, red fills my vision. I rip out of Marco's grip and rush the stage, taking the bag of Botox down.

"You're a fucking traitor." I rip a few clumps of the bleach blond hair from her scalp and manage to get a couple of punches in before I feel a pair of hands pulling me back.

"Enough, *Chiquita*." His hot breath crawls along my skin like a snake, causing my body to shudder.

Lola stands up and rights herself. There's no stopping the smile that spreads over my face at the damage I've inflicted. Her hair is a matted mess as blood drips down her nose. I guess I was able to use Asher's lessons after all. She wipes at her face and spits out a mouthful of blood near my feet. "You've always been such a dramatic little bitch."

"Knew you were a crazy bitch, Charlee, but fuck me I'm hard as stone just watching that." Marco laughs.

"The two of you were in on this together?"

"Your Papá wouldn't let me have you. He made it clear you were off limits. I thought after we offed *tu mamá* he'd see reason, but if anything, it made him hang onto you even tighter."

"You son of a bitch." I twist out of his hold and spin around to face him, but before I can manage a punch, he has his gun up and pressed against my forehead.

"I always get what I want." His black eyes stare back at me, devoid of any emotions. "Lola was my way in, a distraction until I could get him out of the way, and there's not a chance in hell he could resist pussy that sweet if it was thrown his way." He licks his lips as his eyes do a once over of my body. "I know I couldn't." His eyes flicker toward the stage. "Show her what I like."

She winks at me, but her words are for Marco. "Anything for you, baby."

"Pay attention, *Chiquita*. Your only purpose now is to please me," he whispers against my ear, inciting a wave of nausea that rumbles around inside of me. "Sinematic" by Motionless in White blares through the speakers as Lola works the pole for the entertainment of the room, and he forces me to watch. "The game was simple, *Chiquita*. She got your father's money and I got you. Long live the king."

"Fuck you! You'll never be half the man my father was." I spit at him.

His free hand strikes out, slapping me across the face. Kelsey's screams barely register in the background as the metallic taste of blood fills my mouth. "That's the last time you disrespect me, *Chiquita*."

I dab at my bottom lip to ease some of the burning sensation. Pain explodes on the side of my face, but I refuse to cower. If he expects me to whimper and beg, then he'll be waiting a long time. I stand with my shoulders square and meet his gaze head-on.

The man wearing the dress shoes comes forward, clapping his hands and laughing at our little display. "I really like her spirit." His eyes dart to Marco. "Such a waste for you to break it."

"Fuck off, Eddie." Marco doesn't share in his amusement. He moves to hit me again but never gets the chance.

The lights go out and all hell breaks loose.

CHAPTER THIRTY-FIVE

CHARLEE

Two SHOTS RING OUT.
One.

Two.

The backup lights come on, and all I see is blood. Blood everywhere. The bald guy who was holding Kelsey is slumped over the table bleeding out, but Kelsey is missing. Marco's lifeless body is lying on the floor near my feet with a bullet hole in the middle of his forehead and lifeless eyes staring off into nothing, and Lola's dead body is sprawled out on the stage.

I open my mouth to scream, but there's no time for me to react or even make a run for it. A pair of rough hands grab me by the throat, and I'm shoved back against a rock hard chest.

"Don't fucking move, Charlee," Eddie grunts in my ear as he uses me as a human shield. He holds his gun out in front of him with his other hand and whips his gaze back and forth, scanning the room for any sign of Asher, keeping me right in front of him, but comes up empty. The spotlight is shining in our faces and making it hard to see much of anything.

"Let her go." My heart pounds against my chest at the sound of Asher's voice. He's really here.

"Make me." Eddie's laughter vibrates against the middle of my back.

"Six years, Eddie. Six years of swallowing the bullshit only to find out that you're the one who took it all away from me."

"You were getting too close, *Amigo*. I already killed my last partner when he realized Benny was really working for me. Another one would raise suspicion. It was much cleaner this way." Eddie shrugs like he didn't destroy Asher's life.

"Why, Ed? Tell me why you did it? You had dinner at my fucking house for Christ's sakes."

"Money. What else? It's the root of all evil." Eddie's fingers dig deeper into my shoulder the longer he searches Asher out. A noise sounds off to our right and he fires off a shot into the dark.

"You missed, *partner*." Asher's voice sounds much closer this time. He's taunting Eddie, toying with him like a predator does with its prey right before it attacks.

"No more games. Come out right now, or I'll put a bullet in her fucking head." He sniffs my hair and groans. "And it'd be a fucking shame for history to repeat itself because she's a hot piece. Don't you think?"

Asher charges from the darkened corner of the room, knocking us to the ground. "You took everything from me, Eddie. And now I'm going to take from you."

I manage to roll away from them as they start wrestling around on the floor. My eyes scan around the darkened room for a way to escape, but I'm wedged into a tight corner between the stage and the bar with nowhere to go. I'm stuck like a sitting duck and forced to watch them fight it out. I've never felt so helpless.

Eddie attempts to bring the gun up to Asher's face, but Asher slams his hand down against the floor repeatedly until it falls from his grasp. Eddie grunts, but manages to slug Asher in the side of the head. Asher falls back, losing his balance, and Eddie takes advantage.

He jumps to his feet and dives for his gun, but Asher's just as quick and kicks the gun a few feet in front of them.

Both of them end up face to face with their fists raised in a boxing stance. Asher's blue eyes are sizing him up and waiting him out.

"Let's see if you're still as tough as you were, old man."

Eddie lets out a hollow laugh as they bob and weave. "Cyrus should have killed you the first time I told him to, but the dumb fuck wanted to play with his food first and he ended up screwing me." His right hook manages to nail Asher across the cheek.

"I'm going to kill you." He gets a few more hits in before Eddie manages to gain the upper hand and knocks Asher upside the head with the butt of the gun.

I pry myself up off the floor and creep backward in search of an exit, but don't make it very far.

"You're not going anywhere, Charlee." Eddie has his weapon aimed in my direction. All of the commotion fades into a shroud of silence as I stare down the barrel of his gun. My body freezes in place and my feet refuse to budge. I lift my hands in surrender, doing my best to slow my racing pulse.

"Leave her out of this." A muscle jumps in his cheek, but that's the only hint of emotion on his face. "This is between you and me."

"You never could resist being the hero, could you? And that's your biggest weakness." Eddie cocks his gun back and tilts his head. "I'm sorry about this. I really am, but I've come too far to have it all turn to shit." His finger pulls back on the trigger and my heart stops. This is it. This is how I die.

The ear piercing sound is nothing compared to the pain that explodes inside me the moment the bullet tears through my stomach. Blood fills my vision. Like a kaleidoscope of color, it seeps into the material of my shirt. My legs give out from under me as I fall to the ground.

"No!" Asher aims his gun at Eddie and empties the chamber into him as I hear Kelsey scream my name.

Footsteps thump against the ground, stopping near my head as I stare up at the black ceiling. Kelsey drops to her knees next to me, her face a pale and bruised mess. She blurs in and out of focus as the burning of my insides overtakes me. "Charlee, no!" Tears spill down Kelsey's cheeks as her body lies against mine and trembles.

I attempt to lift my hand to comfort her, but it doesn't move. It's like I'm having an out of body experience and watching what's happening to me with no sense of control.

"She's dying! You have to help her, please." Her head lifts as she pleads with Asher, who's kneeling on the other side of me with his hands in my wound to stop the bleeding.

Axel kneels behind her and peels her off me. "It'll be okay, Wildcat."

"No!" Her red hair is plastered to the side of her face as she jerks out of his grip, up to her feet, and shoves a finger in his face. "You stay the hell away from me. This shit is all y'all's fault. She'd be fine if it weren't for you. Any of you! I hate you. You hear me? I hate all of you." She breaks down into hysterics as she watches Asher struggle to save me.

Axel clenches his jaw as his blue eyes harden at her words, but he never takes his eyes off her.

"Kels—" I want to assure her I'll be okay, but my tongue struggles to move. It's becoming weightless and sticking to my mouth.

"Don't try to speak, Charlee. Let's focus on you." Zane's blue eyes meet mine as he kneels on my other side and helps Asher apply pressure to my stomach. I'm not sure where he came from, but I'm grateful he's here, nonetheless.

Numbness begins to fill my limbs as my muscles struggle to function. Things fade in and out of focus the heavier my eyes grow.

"No. Stay with me, *Princess.*" Asher squeezes my hand, bringing me back to the present. Seeing him like this is breaking my heart. Despite what's happened, he's a good man, and I don't know when it happened, but my feelings for him have changed—morphed from hate and anger into something much more. Love.

"I love you." The words come out on a soft wheeze as I struggle to breathe, but I need to get them out because they very well could be my last.

"I love you too, Princess." He bends down and places a soft kiss on my lips. A tear slides down my cheek at hearing those words. He's been my enemy, my nightmare, and now my salvation. I stare into his blue eyes until everything fades into an ocean of nothingness. It swallows me up and carries me away like an undertow, out to a sea of the unknown, and I simply float along in peace.

EPILOGUE

TWO YEARS LATER...

WEEDS COVER THE MARBLE SQUARE. They're overgrown and cover part of her name, but somehow I'm still able to find it. Rain beats down against my back, as I kneel down and pull them out with my free hand, while I tighten my grip on the flowers and teddy bear with the other. Clumps of mud drop over the top of it as I do. I brush them away and stare down at the letters that have haunted me for so long—her name. The tip of my finger traces over the cold wet stone in slow circles.

"You deserved better. So much better than—" I swallow the lump in my throat and suck in a deep breath before continuing. "I just want you to know that I'm sorry. I am so fucking sorry." Tears brim up in my eyes, but I shove them back as my throat burns from the pain. It feels like I'm talking through shards of glass, but with each forced word, it gets easier to speak. Easier to grieve. "The scars are mine to bear and I won't ever forget you—either one of you." I pull out the Saint Christopher medallion from my back pocket and set it on top of the black marble. It still has bits of Luis' dried blood on it, but that's poetic justice to me. My head hangs, as images of our time together fill my head. Every moment I had with her was one I'll never forget, right up until the night I lost her.

A baby cries, bringing me back to the present, and my heart soars at the sound. I set the bouquet of lilies and the blue teddy bear down on the headstone before getting to my feet.

"I'll take her." My hands cradle her tiny body against my chest, planting a soft kiss on the top of her head. The familiar scent of her lavender shampoo gives me some comfort. She has my brown hair and her mother's green eyes. "It's all right. I've got you, Lily pad." I could hold her all day. She's the brightness in the dark that's healing the cracks inside of me.

Like the clouds can read my thoughts, the rain stops, letting the sun shine through. I glance up and let the warmth flood my body. It's almost like she's here with me, encouraging me to be happy.

"What about Mommy?" Charlee smiles up at me as she puts her arms around my waist. We were lucky that night at Viper's Den. The gunshot missed all of her major organs and her recovery was quick. Thank fuck, because we conceived Lily about a year after that.

It's been a couple of months since she gave birth to our daughter and she looks as gorgeous as the first day I saw her. The weight she gained isn't completely gone, but I'm enjoying this curvier side. There's more to grab onto and her ass fits my hands perfectly. I can't wait to knock her up again, but I should probably ask her to marry me first.

"I've always got you, Princess." My free hand wraps around Charlee's neck, pulling her in deeper against my side. I press my lips down on hers and absorb all of the calm she brings me. She smells like rain and home, a scent I will spend the rest of my life craving. A scent that fills the blackened cracks of my soul with light.

"She may want you now, but I'm her favorite uncle," Axel interrupts like the cockblocker he is.

"What? No way." Zane's head whips around. "I'm her favorite. I read to her."

Axel grins and slugs him in the shoulder. "Yeah, but I'll teach her how to shoot."

Lily isn't even one yet and she has us all wrapped around her tiny finger.

Charlee places a hand on my chest and watches them, wearing a devilish grin. "Wait until she starts dating."

Both of my brothers pale and their blue eyes grow wide as they share a look. "That's never happening," they say in unison. And I agree. It's not. No fucking way. No one is good enough for my little treasure.

Charlee laughs and wiggles out of my arms. She steps up to my brothers and playfully taps their cheeks. "I can't wait to watch you tell her that."

She heads off in the direction of the truck with Zane in tow. Ever since that night at the club, my brothers have been more protective of our girls and it's something that helps me sleep much easier at night.

Axel hangs back next to me, his gaze fixed on Lily. I know what he wants even before he asks. "Did you find her?"

"Here." I pull the paper out of my back pocket and hand it to him. "She's living in California under a new name. You sure about this, Ax?"

His blue eyes glare at me. "What would you do if it were Hellcat?"

I nod, knowing damn well what I'd do if it were Princess. "Then bring her home. Charlee misses her, too."

"No other option." He shoves the paper in his pocket and strolls toward Charlee and Zane, but I stop him.

"And, Ax. Do it quietly."

He eyes me for a few seconds, understanding dawning on him. We have a new career path now, one that was carved out of necessity and has become our own version of justice for those less fortunate.

His face lights up in a smile that means my words don't mean shit. "We're Savages, brother. We go in, fuck shit up, and save the day for those who can't. It's what we do now." He winks and continues walking to the truck.

I stand back with my daughter, now sleeping in my arms, enjoying the view. My world is set right. Everything I ever needed is standing right in front of me. With a smile, I turn and walk away, closing the door on my past. I won't ever forget Lauren or our son, but what happened that night doesn't define who I am anymore. The pain is gone.

Replaced with something better.

Something much sweeter.

Peace.

ACKOWLEDGMENTS

THIS BOOK TOOK A TOLL on me emotionally, but it was such a crazy ride that was worth every bit of it. Thank you to Z and my gingers, for keeping me grounded and always encouraging me to never give up, even though I threaten to take a sledgehammer to my laptop daily.

Thank you again to my girls, Lisa and Christy, without you constantly pushing me to not throw in the towel this book would have been sitting in the trash bin. You two were my rock as I treaded through these dark waters and I love your faces so much. My betas— Evelyn, Christina, Shelby, Naomi, Tre, Shelby, and Julia— thank you so much for all of your feedback. I'd be lost without you. To Gwyn, thank you so much for taking the time to help me with all of the legal stuff and making sure it was accurate. To all of the bloggers who took the time to share and read my words, y'all are loved and appreciated more than you know. To my editor, Heather, thank you for always making sure my grammar is spot on. (Obviously, she hasn't seen this page;) Thank you to Ellie McLove, for double checking my ass and making sure I didn't miss anything.

And lastly, I need to do a big shout out to but you, the reader. Thank you. Thank you. Thank you. Without you, the voices in my head would remain just that. You were brave enough to take a chance on my crazy world and for that, I am forever grateful. I hope you enjoyed reading about these characters as much as I enjoyed writing them.

ABOUT THE AUTHOR

Christine Besze is a writer, reader, mother, wife, and lover of all things wine. She lives in her own world of crazy most days, because the voices inside her head hold some great conversation. When she does have to come back to reality and act like an actual grown-up, she spends her time with her handsome hubby Z, their two gorgeous gingers and their mini-herd of German Shepherds. Born in sunny Southern California, she now lives with her family on the East Coast and couldn't be happier. You'll still find her in flip-flops—with a full glass of wine—all year round.

If you enjoyed this story and would like info on future release dates, or just want to see what kind of shenanigans she's up to.

READERS GROUP: CHRISTINE'S CRAZY CREW

f facebook.com/authorchristinebesze

🐦 twitter.com/Cbesze

📷 instagram.com/authorchristinebesze

BB bookbub.com/profile/christine-besze

a amazon.com/author/christinebesze

OTHER BOOKS BY
CHRISTINE
BESZE